I0623016

WILD THINGS

FOUR TALES

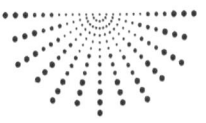

DOUGLAS CLEGG

ALKEMARA
PRESS

CONTENTS

ALSO BY DOUGLAS CLEGG

Want signed and inscribed editions?
Visit DouglasClegg.com/signed-books

STAND-ALONE NOVELS

Afterlife

Breeder

The Children's Hour

Dark of the Eye

Goat Dance

The Halloween Man

The Hour Before Dark

Mr. Darkness

Naomi

Neverland

You Come When I Call You

NOVELLAS & SHORT NOVELS

The Attraction

The Dark Game (Two Novelettes)

Dinner with the Cannibal Sisters

Isis

The Necromancer

Purity

The Words

SERIES

THE HARROW SERIES

Nightmare House, Book 1

Mischief, Book 2

The Infinite, Book 3

The Abandoned, Book 4

The Necromancer

Isis

THE CRIMINALLY INSANE SERIES

Bad Karma, Book 1

Red Angel, Book 2

Night Cage, Book 3

THE VAMPYRICON TRILOGY

The Priest of Blood, Book 1

The Lady of Serpents, Book 2

The Queen of Wolves, Book 3

THE CHRONICLES OF MORDRED

Mordred, Bastard Son

COLLECTIONS

Lights Out: Collected Stories

Night Asylum

The Nightmare Chronicles

Wild Things

BOX SET BUNDLES

Bad Places (3 Novels)

Coming of Age (3 Dark Novellas)

Dark Rooms (3 Novels)

Criminally Insane: The Series (3 Novels)

Halloween Chillers

Harrow: Three Novels (Books 1-3)

Harrow: Four Novels (Books 1-4)

Haunts (8 Novel Box Set)

Lights Out (3 Collection Box Set)

Night Towns (3 Novels)

The Vampyricon Trilogy (3 Novels)

With more new novels, novellas and stories to come.

WILD THINGS

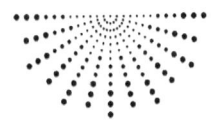

Grandma, what sharp teeth you have!

When Red Riding Hood goes into the cottage, the wolf's deception is near-perfect. The wolf is her grandmother, as far as Red's concerned. Although Red notices the physical change, she believes this is granny. In fact, if the wolf did not reveal itself by saying, "The better to eat you with, my dear," Red might've sat down and brought out some cookies and milk and checked to see if granny wanted a paw rub.

What this led me to believe as a child was that, sometimes, the wolves are closer to you than you think.

More recently, I've come to understand that the problem of wolves is that they tell us who they are, and they bite us. And still we invite them in.

The wolves come down from the mountains when they see the sheep in the pen. If the shepherd does not guard the flock, and if the sheep-dog does not stare down the wolf, then the pen is destroyed, the flock is slaughtered. How often do we leave the gate open to the wolves?

I have come to know the wolves; and the sheep whose eyes are half-closed; and the shepherds and sheep-dogs among us who must be vigilant against those wolves of life.

This is a mini-collection of four stories, two of which are previously unpublished prior to this edition. One among them is a novella.

Each of these four tales, in some way, explores the wild things of life -- the predators and prey, and those who come between them as well as those who are caught in the predator's traps.

The most obvious example is my story, "The Wolf," which launches this collection. It is a fable disguised as a suspense story, wrapped up into a tale of horror. It is not about a shepherd, but about a man and a boy who go up a mountain to hunt a wolf.

In the story, "A Madness of Starlings," there are no obvious wolves, but there *is* the instinct of the narrator to guard against the predators of life.

"The American" is a story about a human wolf. I set it in a cafe in Rome, recalling times in my early twenties when I spent long nights with old friends and new friends wandering the streets of Washington, D.C., Paris, New York, West Berlin or London when we were all young and callow and feckless.

On any given night, I'd be at a table with an Italian man, a French woman, a British couple, a young woman from Mexico, a South African guy, and two Canadians from opposite coasts. Often, their names got lost in a haze and swirl of the potions and poisons of youth. We would go to clubs or just sit at outdoor cafes. The night would turn to dawn before we'd go home, sleep it off and then hear about clubs or gatherings the following evening in other parts of whatever city we occupied. I miss those days because there was no future to them. There was only the "now." I did not have to be anything other than the American sitting at the table saying the things Americans say.

And then one night at a cafe in Paris, I met someone who was a wolf. How did I know this was a wolf?

We know wolves by what they say, because

it's hard for a wolf to keep silent about its wolfish nature.

Finally, the novella, "The Dark Game" is included here.

Of the four stories here, it is the least restrained and the most violent.

The narrator, Gordon, is disordered in his thinking, so the narrative itself becomes disordered; he's telling the story of his life to someone, although we do not know who it will be until the very end of the story.

I had some misgivings about including it here, but there's something about its narrator's complete acceptance of a savage predatory nature that I find intriguing, at least, in fiction.

Now, head on into the forest to meet the wild things.

Douglas Clegg

THE WOLF

The man and the boy had been tracking the wolf since sunrise, but by the time the moon came up they made camp along the ridge.

"Put your rifle over there," the man told the boy, pointing to a pile of rocks covered with fern. "Always put your rifle as far from you and the fire as possible. Accidents happen when they're too close. We don't sleep with them. The wolf won't attack us. It's sheep he's after, not you. Not me."

The boy at first questioned this, because he liked to have his rifle close to him when he hunted. After a few minutes of consideration, the boy decided that the rancher had hired the man to lead, and he would let him. The boy also had done something he wished he hadn't that afternoon, by shooting at what he thought might be the wolf, but turned out to be a silver fox.

By the fire, after supper, they sat across from each other. "We might have had him at the bluffs," the man said. "He's smarter than us, I think."

"I didn't mean to shoot at it," the boy said.

"It doesn't matter."

"I thought I saw him."

"Foxes can look like wolves, sometimes. Coyotes, too."

"It was a stupid mistake."

"I don't care. You're young."

"I'm the best hunter for a hundred miles."

"I can tell."

"Mister, maybe they pay you money to hunt wolves, but when I hunt, it's for the love of the sport," the boy said. "I can take anything out fast. Once I target it, it's mine and that's the end of it."

"I'm not here to argue with you, son."

"I'm not your son."

They went silent again. After he had relieved himself in the woods, the man checked their rifles, and then felt for the small gun beneath his jacket. The man returned to the fire and saw that the boy still sat there.

"We need to get up before first light," he said.

"How many wolves you kill?" the boy asked.

"What?"

The boy glared at him in the firelight. "How many?"

"Twenty. Maybe more."

"That's not a lot."

"No," the man said. "It's not."

"When I'm your age, I bet I'll have more than twenty pelts."

"I don't keep souvenirs like scalps," the man said. "You need to sleep closer to the fire. Take your coat and anything in your pack. Cover yourself good. In a few hours, it'll be colder than you can imagine."

"I hunt a lot," the boy said. "I know how cold it gets up here."

The man did not sleep much. Just before dawn, he rose and rekindled the fire and drew an old rusty skillet from his pack. He made breakfast with the meager supplies he'd brought.

The boy awoke to the smells, and after a mug of coffee began laughing.

"You look like crap," the boy said.

They wandered off the main trails that morning.

THE MAN SAW evidence of the wolf's passing through a route between narrow rocks. There was blood of fresh kill and the rotting smell of a dead animal in the air as they moved further along through the pines. He motioned for the boy to remain still. The man went up along moss-covered rock, through underbrush, and finally came to a cliff's edge overlooking the valley. He glanced out over it to see the distant lake and the dots that were the ranches below. He saw three whitetail deer in a clearing among the trees just above the rocks where he stood.

He sensed the wolf, yet did not see him.

The boy followed him up the trail. When the boy drew close to him, the man whispered, "He knows we're following him. This is a problem now. Yesterday, he didn't know."

The boy remained silent until they had made camp for the night.

"It ain't my fault."

"No one's blaming you."

"You are. You think I scared him off. When I shot my rifle."

The man continued to peel an apple as he leaned back against his pack. "You can't look for blame all the time."

"It was one mistake," the boy said. "I won three hunting trophies before I was fifteen."

The man glanced at him, nodding.

"I bet they paid you a lot of money to do this," the boy said after a minute. "I bet it's a racket you got. You set wolves free down in the valley. Then, eventually, they hire you."

The man laughed at first, but then saw that the boy meant every word. "There would be easier ways to make a living."

"I just can't figure why they'd hire a stranger when we got a lot of hunters in the valley," the boy said. "That's all I meant."

"What did you do makes you special to that town?" the man asked.

The boy wouldn't tell him. He shook his head and said, "I just hunt. That's all. I can hunt and trap and shoot. I win a lot of trophies at the fairground. I can shoot just about anything. Could since I was a boy. First kill was a rabbit when I was ten."

"Jack rabbit?"

"Peter Cottontail," the boy said.

The man said, "What's the last thing you killed?"

The boy didn't answer.

The man said, "First thing I ever killed was a wolf. I was younger than you. You kill a wolf, you start to understand it."

After that, there wasn't much talk around the fire, and the man chuckled to himself when he rolled over to sleep. They had to sleep close beside each other for warmth. The boy's breathing kept him awake for another two hours.

The next day, they went off toward Needle Heights, the bony points of the mountain that crossed into the mountain range leading up north.

The boy asked him what he smelled in the air, and what signs of the wolf he followed, for the boy could not track as well as the man and knew it.

At twilight, the man told him, "I learned from the old mountain men, when I was a boy. There are ways to track wolves. Different from tracking other· animals. There was a mountain man, half-Cherokee, half-Scot. He was an old man, and he took me out to hunt wolves back in the days when we all hunted wolves. He told me that a wolf that got a taste for sheep would draw other wolves down to the ranches. You have to kill them before they can get back up to their pack. Usually, it's the young males. You see it with them first. Old wolves, they know not to go in the valleys, to the ranches. The young ones just see sheep and want them. We tracked this wolf for nine days, and when we finally cornered him, he didn't seem like a wolf anymore. He seemed like a man. I felt as if I knew him, just like I know you. I saw his eyes and I could almost tell what he was thinking. He wanted what you might want. Yes, you. What a lot of men want. He wanted a bite of it. A piece of it. He had wiles and instinct. He knew that if he found a pen full of sheep he might eat better than if he spent his time chasing deer or rabbit."

"Wolves are like rabid dogs," the boy said.

"You just never met one yet," the man said. "They're smart. When they feel threatened, they attack. When you hunt a wolf, you don't let him know he's being hunted until you absolutely have to do it. You wait. You have patience.

You let him think you're just part of the scenery. Just another wolf, maybe. This wolf.

He's just looking for the sheep and then a place to hide. When he finds the prize sheep, that's the one he wants. He doesn't want the sickly or the scrawny. He wants the best."

"It's funny we kill 'em, then," the boy said. "'Cause that's the way some people are. Some people I could name. Where I live."

"Wolves know each other," the man said. "When I had that wolf cornered, when I was younger than you, that wolf looked at me and knew I was a wolf, too. He'd met his match. Only I wasn't a wolf until that day. I didn't want to take a bite of anything until that day. You think you're a wolf, son?"

"A wolf? No."

"Some people are sheep. Maybe most people. And a few people in a thousand may be the vigilant dog that guards the sheep. Now and then, there's even a shepherd. But whenever a group of sheep are together, a wolf always comes 'round. You can count on it. That's why I get work. I'm an expert at wolf killing. They know it in towns in this region. Somebody talks to somebody, and they call me in and pay my fee," the man said. "And I track the wolf. I don't make errors. I don't let the wolf know he's being tracked. I usually work alone. I make sure the wolf I kill is the wolf that's causing distress for people. I don't just kill wolves because I can. I find the right wolf and I do my business."

"I think all of them should just be killed. Every wolf. They all eventually will come down to the sheep. That's what I think," the boy said.

"That would be wrong," the man said, looking the boy in the eye. "What if a man killed another man? Should all men be killed because that one man did wrong? Of course not."

"We're talking wolves, not men."

"Some men are wolves," the man said.

WHEN THEY HAD CROSSED into the deep forest, the man thought for sure the wolf was near. He motioned for the boy to remain silent and at the ready. The man pointed toward the ramble up ahead, overgrown with dead vines.

He gave the signal for the boy to step ahead of him.

The boy raised his rifle up. He stepped slowly between the rocks and trees.

Breaking the silence, the man said, "I was wrong. It's not him."

The boy glanced back at him. His face gleamed bright red with sweat. "How do you know?"

"It's a bitch," the man said. "Heavy with cubs. I don't hunt like that."

The boy moved forward. The man raised his rifle and shot it into the air above the boy's head.

Birds flew out from the underbrush, and the boy turned around in anger.

AT CAMP THAT NIGHT, the boy said, "You did that to scare me."

The man nodded. "We are after one wolf only. We don't shoot any others."

"How do you know she wasn't the wolf?"

"I know the wolf is male. I know its size. I know the color of its coat. And I know its track. This was not the wolf."

"I say kill them all," the boy said.

"You're not a hunter if that's how you feel," the man said. "You may win a hundred trophies, son, but a hunter does not wish to kill them all."

"I hate wolves," the boy said. "I'm tired. I want to go home. The food is awful. Your coffee's awful. I want to be in my bed. At home."

"I know you do," the man said. "You shouldn't have come with me. But here you are. Make the best of it. We'll have him soon." After a moment, the man asked, "Why did you come?"

"I owe it to him. The rancher."

"What do you owe him?"

"I made a mistake once, on his ranch. With him. I need to make it right."

"Mistakes can be forgiven," the man said. "But it's not good to make them."

The boy's lip turned up into a snarl. "That was a mistake. What you did today. Shooting like that. Warning the wolf. He was probably nearby."

"Everyone makes mistakes."

"I bet when they hired you…"

"They?" the man asked.

"The people in town. The ranchers. I bet when they hired you they thought you'd have this done fast. They sent me to learn from you, I bet. Learn. What I learned so far is you worry about wolves too much."

"I wasn't hired by people. I was hired by a person."

The boy thought about this for a moment, and seemed to chew on it. "The rancher was good to me once, but that changed. Maybe it was the wolf attacking his stock. Maybe it was something else."

"You see him as a rancher. I know him as a man who lost his only daughter."

The boy went silent for several minutes. The man watched him.

Then, the boy said, "Not my fault, either."

"I believe you," the man said.

"I didn't do that to her," the boy said.

"I believe you," the man said. "But he hired me to track this wolf. You came along because he wanted you to know what it meant to track a wolf. That's all."

"She was a good girl," the boy said. "We would've been married if…it doesn't matter. It was an accident."

"I know nothing about her or you," the man said. "I just know I was hired to track the wolf. You are the local boy who has all the hunting trophies. So you came with me."

"I wanted to help him. Her father. To make up for it," the boy said.

"If it was an accident," the man said, "then there was nothing to make up for."

The man glanced over at the rifles, placed beyond the fire, in a ditch between rocks and a rotting log.

The boy began to get up as if he, too, thought about the rifles.

The man drew out the gun tucked under his coat, and pointed it at the boy. "Stay where you are, son," he said.

"You're not tracking the wolf," the boy said.

The man stood up and moved closer to the boy. He whispered to the boy that he should not be afraid.

The boy looked as if he might turn and run at any minute, but the man's whispers were calming. The man spoke about how everything would be all right.

"I didn't kill her," the boy said. "Her father is crazy. I didn't kill her. She decided to do what she did. I had no part of it. I was hunting with my uncles. She thought I had abandoned her. I would've married her. I would've come back. If

I had known. I would have. She was good. She was a wonderful girl. I knew I wanted a girl like that. Any man would. You would've if you had known her. She was like an angel to people. I saw it the minute I laid eyes on her. She was one of the good ones. Not all people are good, are they? But she was. She was a good one."

The man aimed the gun to the side of the boy's head.

"Most people are sheep," the man said. "A few are the dogs that guard the sheep. Now and then there is a shepherd, but they are rare. But there are always wolves. A wolf wants to find the best of the sheep and devour it. That is all a wolf wants to do when it finds sheep. That is all it can do."

AFTER THE MAN bound the boy's hands and legs, he went to get his rifle. He stood several feet back from the boy, estimating where best to make the killing shot.

THE AMERICAN

Quested's, a cafe in the old Fire District, looked out on a triangle of park lined with sculptures and trees.

The barman brought out an espresso, tinged with lemon, on a small round tray. He set the cup down in front of the latest arrival.

The American stared at the small cup for a moment as if deciding whether or not to order something else.

"I tried to kill myself tonight," he announced to the couple at a nearby table.

HE SIPPED his drink and glanced out into the night, not caring if they listened.

"I smoked every cigarette I could find.

Drank everything. I swam in the filthy river and then went to a brothel where the whores were shapeless and ancient."

"Now, that's the way to do it," one woman said, from the table nearest his. "Good for you. Bon voyage."

"So you come to a dark little cafe like the rest of us," said the Italian gentleman beside her, his face lit by candle glow from the table's center. "More drinks, good sir. This time, two shots. I feel lucky tonight."

The barman stood by, a small white towel draped across his arm, an emptiness in his gaze. "We're closing in a half hour."

"Why's that?" the tourist from Scotland asked.

"I have a life, that's why," the barman said.

"It's a lovely night," the Italian said, and then began singing, lightly, a beautiful old song in a reedy voice. The handful of ex-pats and tourists, all of them, smiling; with the exception of the American, who glanced face to face, table to table.

The slender branches of nearby trees, full of summer leaf, waved slightly, then, the breeze died.

The American began laughing.

"What's the joke?" said the woman.

"I want to obliterate myself. Somehow."

"Why's that?"

"I am one of the great unloved."

"You can't be more than twenty-three. You can find love next year."

"I don't think that's how it works. I think it begins at birth and goes from there. Then, one day you just recognize it. You're outside the joke that others get. You're not in on what they seem to connect with."

"You're just inexperienced," she said. Then, turning to her the man beside her, she whispered a few words in Italian.

He whispered back.

She said to the American, "Come sit with us. Would you like a cigarette?"

IN A MINUTE OR TWO, he'd changed seats and sat across from the woman and her friends.

She introduced the young man to the others: the Italian gentleman, and a young couple from Bristol who were only in Rome for a week.

One of the Scottish tourists at the next table began whispering to one of the others as if he knew something about the American.

The woman said, "You look familiar to me."

"I'm here a lot, sometimes. I come late at

night. I suppose I drink too much," the American said.

The woman looked at the older Italian man and smiled. "We like Quested's. So many people come here who speak English. My Italian is still a little rough, but I'm getting better, aren't I, Dario?"

The Italian nodded, "Yes. Every day you mispronounce a new word in my language."

"Oh," she said, nudging him with her elbow. She offered a sorrowful smile to the American. "I'm sorry you're not feeling yourself tonight. But that's what drinking's for."

"Have you ever burned for anyone?" the American asked. "Burned? I have. I do."

"Someone must've broken your heart," the woman said. "Here in Rome?"

"A whore," the American said.

"if you really mean 'whore,' you might be smart not to give your heart where you put your wallet," the Italian said. "But I suspect you exaggerate."

"Well, a whore in spirit."

"All of us should be whores in spirit," the Italian said.

"Darling," the woman said, placing her hand on the Italian's wrist. "Give him a little space to grieve for his lost love. Don't all men call women whores when they've been thrown over?"

"It's a man, not a woman," the American said.

"*Aha*," the woman said. "That explains it. Men are all whores. No exaggeration there."

"*I'm* not a whore," the Italian said.

"Of course you're not. Darling, go get us another drink. The barman's too surly."

After the Italian left the table, the woman — who seemed to the American like every British woman he'd met — leaned over and whispered, "You're gay, then. What's that like?"

The American grinned. "Here we go."

"No, I mean, what's it like to feel the way we — women — always feel, and yet have the same instincts as any man?"

The other woman at the table laughed. "It's true. It must be terrible."

"It's exactly the same," the American said. "Nobody feels differently. We're all looking for love, and we're all messed up at the same time. Some people are meant to be loved. I am not."

"That's ridiculous. Utterly ridiculous. Everyone is meant to be loved. Is this about your mother?"

"What?"

"Well, in my experience, men get screwed up by their mothers because mummy wanted a perfect little husband in the perfect little son. It's incestuous. I see it all the time. Especially with you American boys."

"My mother died when I was three, so I suspect that's not the issue."

"That destroys my theory," the woman said. "Do you really want to kill yourself? I mean, honestly, kill yourself?"

He thought a moment but did not answer. He leaned back, looking up at the tree branches. "It's impossible to see the stars through these trees."

"No, it's not. I see them."

"I can't."

The Italian returned with a round tray of small glasses filled with greenish-brown liquid.

"Here we are," the woman said. "Do you like absinthe?"

"Absinthe-*lootly*."

No one laughed.

He added, "I like everything that's bad for me."

"Maybe that applies to the men you pick. Tell me about this recent love."

"Recent one? My only love."

"Wait. You're joking."

"No, I'm not," the American said. "Before him, I hadn't been with a man."

"With a woman before?"

"A few times. In my teens."

"But this was your first real love. That explains a lot," the woman said. "First loves are dreadful unless you're the one who dumps him. So this was just your learning experience."

"No. He was the only one until he had me do things. But that was all for his benefit. It's over. My life."

"Don't be ridiculous," the woman said. "Here, drink. You'll feel better. You'll burn away those feelings along with a few brain cells tonight."

The Italian began speaking to the barman who stood by.

"He wants to close up," the Italian said. "He has a sick child at home."

"Just one drink to go," the woman said. She raised her glass and sipped. "Do you feel it yet?"

"I feel too much," the American said.

"I mean the absinthe. They say it's terrific for destroying the brain."

"And hallucinating," said the Italian.

"I need hallucination to do what I need to do," the American said. "Here's the thing." He took a few sips. "Here's the thing. He told me he loved me. He made me do things that I wouldn't ordinarily do."

"Like?"

"I'd rather not say."

"I see," the woman said "*Sexual* things."

"And other things. He had me…do things. With others. He says it's what will bind us. I was stupid. I don't know who I am sometimes."

The American drank down his glass of absinthe too quickly. "I must be a terrible person. I've done things that I never thought I'd do. I've humiliated myself. I've crossed boundaries I thought I would never cross. For him."

"You'll get sick if you go at it like that," the woman said. "Sip. That stuff'll give you the biggest headache of your life by dawn. And dawn is coming up soon enough."

The Italian took his glass and set it down in front of the American. "For you."

The American glanced up at the Italian. He picked up the glass and took a sip. He kept his nose near the drink as if inhaling something delicious. He watched the Italian as he drank.

"This is a fine drink."

"It's terrible for you. This is really the way to kill yourself," the Italian said. "If you're going to do it. This, or perhaps gelato — or pastries."

The American looked at the glass and swirled the green liquid around in it. "How beautiful."

"This man of yours sounds terrible," the woman said. "Just awful."

"He sounds unusual, that's true," the Italian

said. "But why do these things? Why do what he asks?"

"I love him. I loved him. I still do."

"Love means hurting yourself?"

"Sometimes."

"Did you enjoy any of this wickedness?" the woman asked.

"Enjoy?"

"Well, it sounds like a dirty movie. There must be some fun to it. You were asked to do things you wouldn't ordinarily do. You must like the authority of it. Being told what to do. And doing it."

"I suppose I do like it. And I hate that I like it."

He drank the rest of the Italian's absinthe.

"You've just lost some brain cells," the woman said. "Well, as terrible as that love affair sounds, there are others in the world for you. You're just starting out. There may be dozens of men you'll love before you find that elusive right one."

"I can't do that," the American said. "There's only one man for me. I am not going to live that life, from one to another. I've known people who did that. It is awful. It turns love into a machine."

"But what did this man do to you?" she asked. "He didn't care for you. He used you. No matter how you would like that to be, that's not love. That, my friend, is a machine of some kind. That love of yours." A slight laugh. "It may be fun. It may be a good memory for when you're old and gray and want to think of misspent youth. But it's not love."

"You don't understand," the American said. "Love is about giving yourself up. Body and soul."

"Is it? I thought it was an action. I love Dario," she leaned into the Italian and gave him a squeeze. "But by love, I mean, I do things with him, for him, we have fun, we think about life together. But if he asked me to do something I couldn't do, I'd draw a line."

"Would you?" the Italian began laughing. "Well, I guess I know the limits of our love life now."

"Ha ha," she said.

"No, truly," the Italian said, kissing the top of the woman's scalp and watching the American. "I would draw no line for you. If you wished me to sleep with others, I'd do as you wished."

She swatted at the Italian. "Oh, you. This young man is serious." She leaned across the table and touched the top of the American's hand. "Love is when you trust each other. Like good friends. Best friends."

"I don't think that's love. That's complacency," the American said. "Love is a lot more extreme. It's everything or nothing. I'm not sure trust is part of it."

"That's because you're young."

"You're not old. How old are you?"

"Nearly thirty."

"I bet at twenty you felt differently."

"Perhaps I did. But you grow up." Then, seeing the stricken look on his face, she added, "I think sometimes in life, to learn about love, you have to break at first. You can't have those illusions you have when you're a child. And you will break, first, before you find out what love is. You break and are hurt. As you are now. But then you mend and grow stronger, and you come to realize what love is and what it isn't. And you avoid what looks like love, but is really just some wild animal that has no love in its soul."

"I want to burn from love," the American said.

The woman took a sip from her glass and then lit up a cigarette. "This is such a serious topic. We should talk of lighter things."

"All right," the American said. "How about the war?"

"Oh, no, let's go back to your sex life."

The American, his eyes glazing a bit from

the drink, looked at his glass as if he could see the past in it.

"He had me sleep with soldiers, several at a time. Then, with the wife of a friend."

"A woman?"

"Yes. Then, one night, a man of seventy. He had me steal from people. Just to see if I would obey him."

The woman inhaled deep from her cigarette. "You're taking the piss now. This sounds made up."

"It's not," the American said. "I did it for him. I'd do anything for him."

"Well," the woman said, glancing at the others. "Then you need to separate from this person forever. You need to go get some help."

"Did he make you kill anyone?" the Italian asked.

❧

THE AMERICAN DIDN'T ANSWER.

The woman and the Italian glanced at each other. The other couple began to talk about going home for the evening, back to their flat that was a quarter mile away.

After they left, the Italian said, "I think you're troubled. I think this love you talk of is very disturbing for you. Perhaps you just need to sleep."

"Who can sleep?" the woman asked. "I can't. Not until I put myself out with these." She lifted her glass, then noticed that the American's was empty. "More? Look, Tina's left some in her glass. Have it."

She passed the glass over to the American.

"You asked me if I ever killed anyone for him," the American said. He drank the absinthe down. "'Not yet' is my answer. But I would."

"Would you? That's terrible," the woman said.

"I know. I'm lost. That's why I tried to kill myself tonight. I want to end it. I am never going to be loved. I am not going to ever have him again. I know it. I know it."

"Did he ask you to kill someone?" the Italian asked.

The American glanced at the woman, then at the Italian. "He's out of my life."

"But he did ask you?"

"Yes. But I don't think I can."

"Why not?"

"Dario!" the woman said, giggling as if she had drunk a bit too much. "Of course he wouldn't kill anyone."

"I'm just asking. It sounds like a fantasy

anyway. Who would have this young man sleep with an old man — or with soldiers — who loved him? Who would do that?" the Italian said. "What kind of man? I don't believe he exists."

"He does," the American said. "And I'd do everything I did again. And then some."

"But not kill, I hope."

"I might. I might. I think everyone is capable of killing someone."

"I'm not," the woman said.

"You just haven't met the right person who needed killing," the American said.

"Why do this? For *love*? What does that mean?"

"It means I have no other choice."

"How are you going to kill?" the Italian asked. "If you decide to do this. Hand to hand?"

"That's what he wants. He told me who. He told me where and when. He wants me to use my bare hands."

"You don't seem that strong," the Italian said. "You don't look like you could kill a man."

The American glared at him and slipped a cigarette between his lips.

The Italian leaned forward with his lighter and lit up the American's cigarette.

The woman glanced at the two of them as if she were capturing the moment in some mental photograph. The way the American cupped his hand around the Italian's hand, encircling the heart of the flame as it touched the tip of his cigarette.

"Who did he ask you to kill?" the woman asked, a slight anxiety in her voice.

"Someone I don't know. Someone I don't care to know very well."

The Italian closed the lighter and drew back in his chair. He glanced out into the dark morning. "What I love about the night is that we're all alone in it, even if we're together. Like this."

The woman went silent for a bit. Then, after a minute or two she said, "You should get away from this man completely. You should leave Rome. Go to Paris. Go back home if you need to. Stop drinking. Stop taking whatever drugs you take. Go discover life. There's more to life than love, anyway. You don't need to burn from love, or even burn from liquor. You need some rest and to get away from this terrible human being."

"I don't think I can live without him," the American said.

The woman glanced at the Italian, who still looked out at the night. Then, at the American. Then, to her empty glass.

The barman came out and told them that he was closing up whether they stayed at the tables or not. "I don't have this endless night that you people have."

"All right, all right," she said. "Let's go."

"We can't leave this young man here," the Italian said.

"Oh yes, we can. Do you need a taxi?"

The American stared at her but didn't answer.

She stood up and reached into her purse for money. "You need sleep is all." She said this indirectly. It could've been to anyone — the Italian, the American, the barman, or even to herself.

The Italian remained in his chair but looked up at her. "We can walk down to the fountain."

"No," she said. "Let's go home. Back to my place."

"Let's go to mine," he said.

The American stared at them both, and the woman was nearly certain that tears rolled down his cheeks. She drew a tissue from her purse and passed it to him. "It'll be all right. Whatever it is."

The American took the tissue, swiping it around his eyes. "I've never killed anyone before."

"And you don't have to. Don't talk nonsense. Please."

The Italian finally rose, pushing his chair

back. "You shouldn't have been drinking the absinthe," he said. "It's not good."

"Let's go," the woman whispered, loudly enough for the American to hear.

"All I'm saying," the American said. "All I'm saying is that I'm thinking of killing for him. That's all. I don't know why he drives me to this. I don't know what he wants. I only know I have to do what he wants."

The Italian stepped back from the woman and nodded. "Love is a cruel thing, sometimes. It needs proof. These are dangerous times in the world. We've met an assassin over drinks at Quested's."

As she passed by the American on her way out, the woman said, "Just go home and go to sleep. It'll seem different when you wake up."

She nearly touched him on the shoulder as a way of comforting him but withdrew her hand at the last second.

The woman and the Italian gentleman left Quested's, walking out under the trees, through the park.

As she stepped into the path between some thin sculptures, she shrugged off the touch of the Italian as if she were annoyed with him.

AFTER A MINUTE, the American got out of his chair, as well. The lights of Quested's shut off and the barman went home.

The American stepped into the park and moved through the shadows to catch up with the couple.

A MADNESS OF STARLINGS

Wh

hat possessed me to retrieve the little fledgling, I can't say for sure. I rescued the baby bird from the jaws of the tiger-striped tomcat that had been stalking it. I wanted to show my boys that the smallest of life sometimes needed protection from the predators.

I brought it into the house, hoping to wait out the cat's bloodlust. My two boys came out to look at it. I warned them not to touch the bird just then. "The less contact it has with people, the better."

After an hour, I took the bird outside again. My kids watched from the living room window.

It hopped in the tall summer grass that I had not gotten to with the mower. Its mouth opened wide, up to the skies, expecting its mother to come with food.

I stepped back onto the porch and scanned the area to make sure no cat returned. I hoped that the bird's mother would return and feed it so that the balance of nature could be restored and I'd have no more responsibility.

An hour later, the fledgling continued to hop and squawk and open its mouth to heaven. No mother arrived. I had lost my own mother when young, and did not like remembering this when I saw the bird I came to call Fledge. Loss was the bad thing in life. I hated it, and didn't wish it on a baby bird.

I took the little guy in, and my wife, Jeanette, and the boys (little William and tall Rufus) helped me build a cage for it as part of our "Saturday Family Project." At first, Fledge would not eat from my hand — or from a straw. But we picked up some mealworms and crickets from the pet store in town, and soon enough, the little guy hunted them up on the floor of his cage.

Devouring fifty worms a day and perhaps ten crickets, Fledge grew fast.

WITHIN FIVE DAYS, the little guy had full feathers and the boys and I took him into the rec room from flight training. He flew from Rufus' fingers to the bookcase.

I had to put a stepladder up to rescue him from the highest shelf.

"We have to let him go," I told the boys. "He's ready to fly. He's eaten a lot and knows how to catch crickets and peck for worms on his own."

"Isn't he a pet?" William pleaded. "He's ours now."

Rufus, the elder at nine, added, "He can't survive out there, Dad. He can't. He's too used to us."

"It's only been a week," I said. "He belongs out there."

"I heard birds only live a couple of years out there," Rufus said. "I bet in his cage, he'd live a long time."

"He's a wild bird, he's meant to be out there. Besides, when we go to Florida in February, who's going to take care of him?

Will you clean the cage for the next twelve years if he lives that long? Every day that cage needs cleaning," I said.

Rufus looked very sad, and William's eyes glistened with the easy tears of a little boy who won't accept loss. "But Daddy," he said. "Daddy, I love Fledge."

"I know," I said. "But don't you want Fledge to be happy?"

William nodded. "I want him safe."

"He's happy here," Rufus said. "Now. He won't be happy when a cat gets him. Or when an eagle gets him."

"We don't have eagles around here."

"Or when he gets some disease and nobody takes him to the vet."

"I'm going to miss him," William said. "So long, Fledge."

"Look, he'll be around the yard. He's a starling. They're always here. He'll probably fly around and make a nest under your bedroom window."

William's eyes brightened. A smile crept across his face.

Noticing that I had turned the corner on William's emotional rollercoaster and now things were heading upward, I said, "And whenever you see him hurt, you can run out and bring him in and we'll take him to the bird doctor, if you want."

Rufus had begun to scowl. "I saw a dead bird out by the curb. That's what's going to happen to him if we let him go."

"Roof," I said. "Roof, look. When you grow up, we're going to let you go. You're going to fly away. And as much as I'd like to put you in a cage here so I can always see you, I know that's going to be wrong."

Of course, he didn't understand this. Rufus felt he'd never leave the house or his parents or the protected world of childhood.

But *I* knew he would.

I knew the bird needed to get out and live just like my kids would one day need to get out and spread their wings. Even when the tomcats of life got them.

The shelter of childhood was temporary, at best.

The boys put up more protests, with Rufus cataloguing the bleak prospects of a bird in our suburban world. I countered his arguments with tales of birds flying over the treetops, or Mother Nature, or how Fledge saw us as giant monsters that were not like his parents or brothers and sisters. "Starlings have to fly twenty miles a day to really enjoy life."

Finally, I let the discussion die down. When the boys were out playing with friends, I took Fledge onto my fingers, and leaned out the second floor window of our house.

The bird flew off.

Just as it got up into the air, clearing an overgrown azalea bush, another bird came down and began attacking it mid-air.

I felt panic and genuine terror.

I worried about the little guy, trying his wings out for the first time. Fledge continued flying toward a crabapple tree in the front yard. Fledge turned, almost as if he were looking at me. His mouth opened wide as he squawked like a baby. In that moment, I didn't see the bird; I saw my boys.

I HAD a premonition of a moment of terror in life when I would let go of my sons' hands and they would go off and the world would do its own version of attack on them. My imagination went haywire as I imagined Rufus in his early twenties in a foreign land, felled by bullets in a war; and William, injecting heroin into his arms, surrounded by lowlife friends in some crack house.

As I watched Fledge, he fluffed up his feathers and spread his wings wide and flew over the rooftop. I raced to the bathroom window, and saw Fledge flying over other houses, off through the neighborhood.

Fledge had made it past the attacking bird. Past the trees. We had done it, I thought. We helped Fledge get strong and healthy and become an adult, and he was going to live his life the way he was meant to live it. My brief insanity, those split-second visions of my boys, the dreadful futures I imagined for them — all of it dissipated and I laughed at myself and the way my mind worked.

Later, I told the boys that Fledge had flown off, and that he was fine. They moped a bit, but the more we talked about Fledge and Fledge's life, the better my children seemed to understand why Fledge had to go.

That first night, I went and sat in front of Fledge's empty cage. Beyond the cage, a window looked out on trees. I opened the window and lifted the screen. Part of me felt that Fledge might come back, or if he was hurt, he might show up for food again.

I kept the window open for three days, and then shut it.

I MISSED THE BIRD.

We had kept the little guy for five days, but it was enough for me to begin to think about life and nature and to wake up each day hoping Fledge had not died in the night. Out the window, other starlings and robins and mock-ingbirds flew around, but I kept watch for

Fledge. I brought out the old binoculars from the cabinet in the garage, and, early in the morning — before even my wife awoke — I went to the window and looked out. I whistled sometimes when I was in the yard, thinking Fledge might hear my voice.

Then, at twilight, I spoke to my wife, Jeanette, about the bird.

"It's a starling," she said. "They're nuisances. I bet the state would've paid you to kill it."

"Stop that," I said. "It needed help."

"I know. I'm kidding. Really. I'm kidding. But the bird's fine. Believe me. You protected it. You got the boys to think about nature a little. And now that bird's off doing what birds do."

"I never really noticed starlings before," I said. "I mean, I knew they were out there."

"God, in the fall they just swarm. Freaks me out sometimes. Like the Hitchcock movie."

"I was out in the yard this morning," I said. "I couldn't stop looking in the trees. And on the roof. I just figured he'd stick around."

She gave me a funny look, as if she were trying to figure out if I were joking or not. "Honey? It's a bird. You really want a bird, we'll get a cockatiel. But I don't really want a bird," she said.

"I don't want a bird, either," I said. Then, I

laughed at myself, and she giggled, too. We had some coffee and went out on the patio. We sat in the old deck chairs that were gray from years of neglect. "But it's funny."

"What's that?"

"Loss. All of life is about loss."

"No, it's not." She laughed and told me I had better not get depressed on her.

"Life has loss in it," she said, when she saw that I was a little hurt by her laughter. "But look, we both have great jobs, the kids are great. We're building to something. We have love. There's a lot in life besides loss."

"Someday, we'll lose everything. I mean it. I'm not sad about it. I guess I'm wistful."

"Wistful is sad."

"No it's not. Someday, the boys will go out into the world. Not everyone survives it. God, maybe I'll get heart disease. Or some...some accident will happen."

"You're getting morbid," she said. "I hate this kind of stuff. You shouldn't say it. It's too dark."

"I'm trying to grasp this thing. I'm nearly forty, and I want to be prepared. I want a good mindset."

"That bird," she said. "It got you thinking like this."

"It's nuts, I guess," I said.

"Not nuts, honey. But it's…it's useless. We have a good life. Bad things don't always happen. That bird. That bird is probably off flying around, happy as hell to be out of the cage and back in its natural environment. It's probably flocking with other starlings, devouring someone's grass seed or chasing off squirrels from a nest that it's building with a mate. It's an adult by now. It's fine. That's how life goes."

"Did you hear that?" I asked, startled as I glanced over at her.

She held her coffee mug near her lips, watching me. "What?"

"That sound. Was that Fledge?"

I heard it again. The bickering squawk of a starling. Somewhere among the trees.

"No. Wait," she said. "No."

Then, I heard a chirp at the rooftop. I looked up — it was a sparrow.

"Come here," Jeanette said.

I glanced over at her. She had raised her eyebrows ever so slightly, her version of close-up seduction.

"What for?"

"Just come here." She set her mug down on the little table, and scooched back in her chair. "Sit with me."

"We'll break the chair."

"Throw caution to the wind."

I went over, and she put her arms around me. Kissed me on the forehead. "My big baby who loves birds."

Deftly, she slipped her fingers to the buttons of my shirt, and opened them, her hands going to my chest, combing through the patch of hair. I kissed her, and she whispered, "The boys won't be back from the Nelson's 'til nine. Nobody can see us."

We made love in that uncomfortable deck chair, in that desperate way that old marrieds do, trying to recapture the wildness of premarital sex. Somewhere in the rapture of it all, I heard the chattering of starlings in the trees, and glanced up.

"What is it?" she asked. "Why did you stop?"

"I thought…" I didn't want her to know what I was thinking, so I kissed her on the lips. "Maybe we should do this later."

"Why?"

"I feel funny. What if someone sees us?"

"Nobody can see us."

"I feel like someone can," I said.

"So, we give 'em a show. Greatest show on earth."

"Naw," I said, trying to sound warm and

cuddly and friendly, but I drew my underwear and pants back up, and buttoned my shirt. She left hers open, but drew her knees together.

"Since when do you turn down outdoors sex?" she asked.

"We've never had outdoors sex till now."

"I remember a certain hot August night on a lake in a little boat with life preservers as pillows," she said. "August 18th."

"You remember the date?"

"Sure. We were out at the lake. It was when we…"

She didn't have to finish the thought. It was the year before we conceived Rufus. It was to be our first child, the one who came from sex in the boat out on the lake at midnight. But she had lost the baby within four months. Eight months later, she was pregnant with Rufus.

I didn't like to be reminded of the first child.

THAT NIGHT, after my wife fell asleep, I went out to the patio for a cigarette. My first in three years. I kept the pack of Gitanes in an old backpack I'd had since college. It hung on a nail in the garage. Inside the pack, besides the French cigarettes I'd learned to smoke on a post-graduate trip to Paris, there was a bottle of Grand

Marnier that had never been opened, a T-shirt with various obscenities written on it, and a pair of swimming trunks I had not been able to fit into since my twenties.

The cigarette tasted great, and I followed the first with a second. I thought of Fledge, up in one of the trees, his little leg hidden under his feathers, with the other leg down, small claws clutching a tree branch.

THE FOLLOWING SATURDAY, I took the boys for a hike. First, to a drug store to get some candy, and then up to the unincorporated area of town where there was a bike trail by the old railroad tracks. The boys seemed to have fun, running ahead of me, climbing rocks, finding a penny or quarter, balancing on the railroad ties. But I had begun hearing the birds. I heard more and more of them as we got deeper into the woods. Starlings, certainly, but also the caws of crows; the songbirds, too, with their chirps and whistles. I felt like I would hear Fledge's distinct squawk, but did not, and even while I told the kids to watch out for broken glass on the trail, or not to touch the poison ivy, part of me had blocked even my own children out.

I had never noticed so many birds before.

Most of them were unseen, but their voices seemed loud, even annoying. Bickering in the skies, chattering in treetops, their language must have meant something to them. They must be communicating with each other. Mating. Attacking. Flocking.

Twilight came, and back at home, Jeanette made it bath time for the boys because of the dirt all over their faces.

I went to the second floor bedroom window, and climbed out onto the ledge, and sat on the roof. Smoked a cigarette. Leaned back, and looked up at the veiled sky and the darkening clouds in the distance.

Distinct voices of the birds. Not just the usual cacophony. I felt as if my ears had begun to notice precisely how one sparrow chirped, how the swallows spoke to each other, and those starlings — their nastiness, their territorial voices that spoke of battle and ownership. I began to hear something in the world I'd never really heard before.

"ARE YOU ALL RIGHT?" Jeanette asked that night. We lay in bed. Lights on. She had just put down the book she'd been reading.

"Of course."

"You're staring at the ceiling."

"I'm thinking. You know, there must be something weird about life. We took that little guy in for five days, and now I just notice birds. I've never noticed them before."

"What's that called?"

"What do you mean?"

"It's called something. When you didn't notice something. Then you do. Then you notice it's all around you all the time."

"Crazy?"

She grinned. "No. No. And it's not about something being ubiquitous, either. It's something else. Like when you've never heard a word before, and suddenly, once you've heard it, it's everywhere you look."

"I keep listening for him."

"For who?"

"Fledge."

"Honey," she said. "Aw. Poor baby. I miss the little guy too. You should be proud of yourself. You rehabbed a bird and set it free. That's what life should be about."

"I read about starlings. Online. They're non-native. They were brought here by a guy who released a hundred of them in Central Park in 1890. He wanted to introduce birds that were in

Shakespeare's plays. So he brought starlings, among others. I read that in the wild they don't live all that long. In captivity, they can live up to twenty years."

She lay down and turned to me, her eyes like warm muddy pools. "I would rather have a few years among my own kind, with a life of mating and birth and, yes, even death, than twenty years alone in a cage."

"He wouldn't have been alone," I said. And then, "Aw, this is silly. I'm silly."

"Yes, you are. It's not about the bird, is it?"

"I told you before. It's about loss."

"I know. Life does have a lot of loss in it. You're almost forty. You'll probably start buying sports cars and chasing blondes."

"No. I'm not that guy," I said. "I just hate how life takes everything away."

"That's ridiculous. Think of all the people in the world and what they don't have. Now, think of all that you have. And tell me how life takes everything away from you."

"Not from me, personally. From everyone. Nobody really tells you that when you're Rufus' age. We protect our kids from it. But it's there."

"God. That fucking bird," she said.

She turned away from me, and reached over to flick the light off.

THAT WAS ORDINARY LIFE, but the extraordinary had entered my life through the voices of birds. Whenever I went outside, or opened a window, I heard them. Too many of them. The voices all going on about food and shelter and war and children and work and flight and anger and joy. I could tell that much from the tones of their voices. I noticed that when a storm came, the gulls from the bay — a good hour from us — suddenly were on our rooftop. But then, I began to hear the voices of the birds change when a storm was predicted, as if they knew, many hours before a thunderstorm reached us, that it was going to descend. Any changes in their voices, or the amount of bickering, heralded nestlings. I began to hate crows, for I saw them dive for the babies, and heard the awful wailing of the mother birds at the death of a child.

Then, one evening we watched a TV show on a Wednesday night; it was still light out; I began to hear the birds squawking and thought I heard Fledge, so I went to the window, opening it.

"What's up?" Jeanette asked.

"I heard something."

She turned the television's volume down, and listened. "I don't hear anything. What was it?"

"Nothing," I said. I had begun to lie to her about hearing the birds outside. Listening for Fledge, trying to see if there was a message I should be hearing. That's what I had begun thinking: there was a message that might be delivered to me. Delivered unto me — it had begun to seem religious to me. Birds brought omens. God might speak through birds. I knew that was just my imagination, but something spiritual had entered my life through the sounds of the birds.

I took a day off from work, but didn't tell my family. Instead, I took some binoculars and spent the day up in my sons' tree fort, which nearly went into the thick woods behind our house.

I took water and sandwiches and soda; when I had to pee, I just peed off the tree. I listened all day to the birds, and I began to feel a change within me — toward nature. It made me sad in some way, because I began to see my wife as someone who would never truly understand me, and with whom I might never genuinely communicate what was within me. I loved my boys, but I knew they had other lives to live.

They, too, would develop their own secret languages and matings and lives.

I might never understand them fully as I could never fully comprehend my wife.

I began to take personal days off from work, and just wander the woods, or walk along the bike trail. I'd get lost for hours at a time in the deep forest that should not have been there — for there was a shopping mall two miles away, and a town on either side. Yet, a forest existed, and I could lose myself in it for half a day without seeing another human being.

There were arguments at home that escalated into shouting matches.

I became less tolerant of the boys' behavior when they crossed a line. At work, I just didn't deal with others much and spent most of my time pretending to be buried in projects that I knew I'd never finish. On my lunch break, I'd go out to the park and sit and listen to pigeons and yet more starlings, and watch as they flew and stole bits of food from near the trash cans and dive-bombed someone who sat too close to a hidden nest.

On a bitter day of bad reports at work, and a wife who didn't even want me to come home,

I walked along the bike path in the woods, and could not stand the voices of the birds anymore.

I wept in my wife's arms that night, and told her I had some kind of madness in me. She cooed into my ear and told me she loved me and that it would pass, whatever it was, and if it didn't, we'd get help.

"It's all the loss," she said. "You didn't cry when we lost the baby. You didn't cry when your mother died. That bird did it. It reminded you of loss. It got to you."

The bird had changed me. The bird had never left me. I longed for the kingdom of birds rather than the kingdom of men. The voices of birds seemed, to me, to be more about life than the voices of mankind.

A CALL CAME in to work for me, but I didn't pick up. I just let my voice mail get it, and it wasn't until my wife messaged me on the cell phone that I paid attention.

She wrote:

Emergency Room.

When I got there, she was trembling and pale. I held her, and she whispered, "William."

Strangely, I noticed a man nearby who looked as if he had just done something terrible. He spoke to a nurse and mentioned "birds."

I suppose that was why I noticed him at all. Later, I learned that he had been the one driving the car.

DURING THE SIX months after my son's death, I began to listen only to the birds. I barely acknowledged Jeanette, and though I loved Rufus dearly, I could not bear to look at him for he reminded me too much of his little brother. I smoked my Gitanes in the open now, for my wife could not chide me during this time.

I spent long afternoons and evenings out on a lawn chair, beneath the sycamores and maples, my eyes skyward as I watched the dark flocks of starlings readying for winter. Their words comforted me, and took me elsewhere as they spoke of distant places of warmth and insects. Though I often thought of William's warm fingers in my hand or his soft whisper at bedtime, the birds told me about life and death and loss and continuations and how the spring brought hope and summer brought plenty. I also heard about the deaths of birds, of sorrow, of a mate shot down by a thoughtless boy with a gun, of marriages and the ends of marriages, of wounds that never healed, and feuds between siblings that continued to the end of life.

Laid off from my job by October third — in a massive layoff that left thousands without work — I came home to an empty house. By empty, I mean, bereft, without human voice. Jeanette and Rufus had left a couple of weeks earlier to stay at her sister's in the next town over, but they would be back (so my wife promised) or things would change or something. I wasn't clear on the details.

In the early morning, I went out in my boxers and sat on the back lawn. The earth had turned hard and cold, and the wind was strong. I listened for the birds, and leaned back, my arms crossed behind my head. Still sleepy, I began to doze when a voice brought me up from sleep.

What the voice had said, I am not sure. It seemed like my name or a name. The sound was nearly like a child's voice. Perhaps I had been dreaming that it was my dead son's voice.

I opened my eyes. There, on a slender leafless branch above me, a starling. Dark, and mottled with the yellow stars of adulthood, and — I was sure — it was Fledge himself. Watching me.

"Fledge?" I asked, but then laughed at my foolishness for asking a bird its name.

The bird cocked its head to the left and the right, and then hopped down to the ground. It fluttered over and hopped up on my chest. It began squawking and making a whistling sound that was a fairly good mimic of my own whistle.

Then, it hoped closer to my face.

Instead of a whistle, it spoke to me. "William," said the bird.

As I lay there, stunned by this hallucination, the bird flew away.

Now, of course I thought I had lost my mind, but I had to know something I didn't know before. Something I'd never really asked or followed up on.

I went to visit the man whose car had hit and killed my little boy.

"Yes?"

The door opened, and the man, who I guessed was about fifty, opened the door to his apartment. He lived in a rough neighborhood near the city, but had not lived there at the time of the accident. He had lived, the day when my son stepped off the curb, in a nice house, larger than my family's place, but the death of my son had changed him as much, if not more, than it had changed us. His own life had fallen apart. His wife and he had divorced. He had a grown daughter who blamed him, though it had been apparent that he had been driving the speed limit and had done what he could to avoid hitting my son and several children who had stepped into the street in heavy traffic. He had only hit my son, but four children's lives had been spared, including my eldest, Rufus.

Yet, his life had spiraled downward.

I saw it in the apartment building, which was dark and filthy.

I saw it in his eyes, as well. "Oh," he said, recognizing me. He didn't ask the next question, but it hung there as if he had: What do you want?

"You said something. I barely heard it. I guess I wasn't listening."

He opened the door a bit wider, but looked at me with a kind of anticipation as if I might swing a punch at him. "I'm sorry," he said. "I really am."

"You said something about birds," I said.

"Oh." He looked over my shoulder as if expecting others to be with me. "The birds."

"What was it about birds. I overheard it. We were standing there, at the hospital. But I just caught the tail end of it. I didn't even know who you were at the time."

"I can't remember," he said.

"It's important. To me." Without realizing it, I had begun sobbing, and I suppose my body heaved with each exhalation of grief.

He came out into the hallway, and put his arm around my shoulder. "Come in. I'll get you some water."

INSIDE THE APARTMENT, on a green, worn couch, I sipped from a glass. Vodka, not water. It tasted good.

He sat across from me. Behind him, the television was on, but the sound had been muted. "I don't remember about birds. Look, I'm sorry. I have nightmares about what happened. I see his face."

"Me, too."

"I see all their faces. If I had only...if I had only stopped for the ice cream my wife wanted. If I had just taken the short cut instead of driving down Apple Valley Road."

"I know. I think if I had just made him stay home from school. If I had just told Rufus not to play after school. 'If only' drives you nuts. I'm weary from it."

"Yeah."

"You said something about birds. At the Emergency Room. You were speaking to a nurse."

"Oh," he said. A shadow passed over his face. "Oh. The birds. I saw them. Blackbirds. I think that's what the kids were doing. There was a bird in the street. I saw it, too. Just sitting there, and I thought it was going to get hit by somebody. I think that's why the kids went in the street. Maybe I'm wrong. I don't know." He emptied his glass, and sighed. "Does it matter? I'm sorry. I'll be sorry for the rest of my life."

"It was an accident," I said, and then rose, setting my glass on the glass table.

I WAITED for Rufus after school. When he saw me, he looked at me as if I were the enemy. He walked cautiously to the car, and leaned into the open window.

"Come on, I'll drive you to Mom's."

"She's gonna be mad."

"She'll be mad when she sees me. At least she won't be mad at you."

Driving him to his mother's place — which really was his aunt's large home where they were staying for a few weeks until everything somehow either worked out or didn't — I said, "You doing okay?"

He remained quiet.

"I want to ask about something."

Again, no response from my boy.

"All right. Look. That day. That *day*. Was there a bird? Or a flock of birds?"

He looked at me, his eyes seeming to flash with anger. Then, back to the road ahead. Then, he blurted, "Don't ever talk to me about that day again. I mean it. I never want to think about it."

As I dropped him off at his aunt's house, he slid out of his seat and had not yet swung the door shut. I said, "Just tell me. Why did you go in the street at all? There was traffic."

"Ask William," Rufus said, his face a mask of childhood fury, which was both pale and burning. "He's the only one who knows. I was trying to stop him. I was trying to stop him. Nobody believes me. I was trying to stop him!"

❦

MY WIFE CALLED me on the cell phone ten minutes later and yelled at me for making Rufus upset. She said he had gone all fetal and wouldn't talk to anybody and that if I showed up at his school again she didn't know what she'd do, but she'd do something.

I barely heard her — the birds were talking outside, and I went out to them and tried to decipher what they were saying.

Winter had not quite come 'round the bend, but autumn had exploded briefly like a firecracker and stripped the trees bare.

On the twisted branches, the dark swarms of starlings began chanting.

I STOOD THERE, in awe of them, their beauty and their language and their flight.

They spoke of journeys to sunlit lands, and of love among them, and of the legends of their ancestors and of the anger and fury at the deaths of those they raised up from birth. I wandered back through the yard, into the woods, and followed them.

I, earthbound, watched as they danced tree to tree to sky to telephone wire to rooftop.

I began speaking in the tongues of birds and all else fell away, the whistles and warbles from my throat seemed perfectly natural. The starlings told their secrets to me.

I knew my son's final moments. The starlings told me what they had seen, what my boy

William had done. It was in their songs, their exaltations, their chattering squawks as they surrounded me, a cathedral of dark birds.

They shared with me the love I had taught him for even the smallest bird, the tiniest creature, in the road, to be rescued from the traffic of human monsters. I heard his footsteps on the street as he raced into traffic.

The birdsong grew deafening. I clutched my hands to my ears, for I could not take what they told of my little boy.

I pressed my fingers deep into the skin of my ears — and deeper still to the wax — to plug them up and keep the sound of the last moment's of my boy's life from entering my brain. The pressure was enormous as I pushed my fingers deeper still.

And yet, I heard his voice as he shrieked, and the thud of the car against him — they warbled each note of his last moments of life so that I might feel I was there with him. I begged them to stop, but the birds continued their praise of my little boy. They mimicked his cries and the wheezes of his lungs and throat until he breathed his last.

I felt as if I were there, with William, in the street, his head upon my lap, his eyes turned upward, his small body shivering.

As if I held his small body and looked up to

God in the sky, but only saw the birds that had witnessed his death. The birds that had lured him into the street. The birds that had begun to drive me to madness with their terrible words and sounds.

Their voices, telling me of other secrets, of those who had died in the past, and the deaths to come.

THE DARK GAME

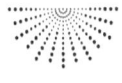

A NOVELLA

I saw a painting in a gallery once that depicted a man's hands, bound together.

Its title: "Victory is Freedom of Mind and Body."

I believe that is true. I would go further and say that victory is freedom of mind *from* body.

Separation from the thing that imprisons us.

Flight.

Perhaps freedom from life itself.

That is victory.

Life is brutal.

It's like this whip and these ropes. It hurts. It scars. But we must take it.

We must find some pleasure and solace within this terrible lashing.

You want to hear it all? You want me to tell

you how it went, in the prison camp? Why I like the ropes?

You want to play the game with me?

First let me tell you this:

Youth is something you put in a drawer somewhere.

You lose the thought of it behind socks and letters and medals and old passport photos and keys that no longer fit locks.

You wear it when you're of the right age, and you do things that you ought not to, and then as you gain perspective with age, you put it away, and you close the drawer.

And you lock it.

Then, you live the life you've built toward, and no one needs to see what's in that drawer.

A secret is something to be hidden.

If is hidden well enough, it never becomes a fact. It is just something that is not there when you go to look for it. It is the thing missing, but the thing that is not missed.

That's how I feel.

That is why I don't revisit those times, often.

The camp.

Or the motel room.

Or the smokehouse.

But since you have me here, like this, I'll tell you.

Maybe you'll leave after that. Maybe you

won't want to stay here once you know about me.

§⬧

BEFORE THE WAR, I was in a motel room with a girl I met outside the base.

For fun she tied me up and when she did it, I went someplace else in my head. My hands tied, my feet bound. I remember she smelled like orange blossoms, and she enjoyed tightening the thin ropes around my hands.

But my mind was just gone – drifting upward into darkness, into another place. Back to Burnley Island, I guess, and that's where I've always ended up – *my memories, my family, my home.*

I was just not there anymore. The game had taken me over.

It had become automatic for me.

It was second nature.

In the war, things got worse for me.

The game got worse.

But it wasn't so bad when I was a kid.

§⬧

EARLY MEMORY:

Winter.

Bitter cold.

Wind whistling around me, boxing my ears, as I trudged through three feet of snow to get out to the smokehouse. I was ten, perhaps. Heavy with a burden.

It was the dog I'd had since he was a foundling of two or three years old, and I was too young to remember bringing him home from a walk in the woods.

He was dying now, of some undiagnosed malady. In those days, you didn't take the dog to the vet when it was its time.

You took him someplace and you shot him.

And this freezing February day, that was what I was to do.

My father marched behind me. I could not bring myself to turn and look over my shoulder to see how he kept pace. I was weeping, and it would be the first and last time I would weep for years.

I held my dog – a small mutt, no bigger than my arms could carry – and he looked up at me as if he understood that something not wonderful was to come.

At the smokehouse I stopped and prayed. I wished that God would intervene, just this once.

I would trade, I promised God, my life for

this dog's. I would do anything God wanted me to do if he would just take a minute and breathe new life into my dog's body. I would build a chapel.

No, I would build a *cathedral*.

The snow bit at my cheeks and nose.

MY DOG, whose name was Mac, whimpered and groaned.

"Go on, son," my father said.

He called me "son" more than he ever used "Gordie" or "Gordon."

Sometimes I thought he wasn't sure of my name. That I was just another son to him. Another child to deal with before I became a man.

I reached up, and opened the door to the smokehouse. I barely kept my balance, for the dog had grown too heavy for me.

My father lit the lantern inside the building – the smokehouse was old-fashioned, and my mother felt it was a fire hazard, but my father insisted on using it.

A yellow flickering light filled the small room.

After I set Mac down on some straw, I kissed him on the muzzle and kept my prayers going – my deals with God to change this, somehow.

Then, my father handed me the pistol and told me to get it over with quickly.

"Misery is terrible. That animal is in misery. When you brought him home, you promised to take care of him. That is a commitment. This is a way to take care of him, so he won't be in any more pain. You can stop his pain. He won't get better, son. He won't."

"I can't," I said.

"You have to. You promised. You promised me. And you promised that dog when you brought him home. He has had a good life here. But now he's sick. And he needs to be taken care of."

I looked at my dog's face and saw the terribleness of all existence in his eyes. In his shivering form.

And that is when I learned about how life doesn't matter at all.

Not one bit.

It is a misery. A wretchedness foisted on us by a God who turns His back on all.

We live on a planet of ice, and the only thing we human beings can do is endure it and try to make sure that we don't add to the misery too much.

Here is my life:

I was born on Burnley Island, in a house called Hawthorn, and I grew up in a family called Raglan that had a history on that island.

We were shepherding people, I'm told, originally. We came with Welsh and Scots and English in our blood, and we were dark and swarthy, as I am, a perfect descendant of the Raglan clan.

My father was a brute, and I don't say that lightly. He was a man more likely to lash with a belt or a switch than to scold with words. He was quick to judge, and hot tempered, and I suppose I joined the army to get away from him more than anything else.

I went off to see the world and fight the good fight, and found myself one dawn in the heat of a jungle, in the boredom of a company that was lost, our communications screwed beyond all measure, and I had a "fuck all" attitude toward the war and the jungle.

I was nineteen, and the last place I wanted to be was in that miasma of heat, humidity and the stink of swamp.

And then, before much time had passed, the enemy got us.

No need to go into specifics.

It was ugly.

There were a dozen of us originally, but by the time I regained consciousness, tied like a pig to a stick, there were only eight or so – counting me and my buddy, Gup (short for Guppy, which was a kinder name than his original nickname, which was Shrimp), Davy, who seemed too young to be a soldier, a man I had no liking for (named Larry Pastor), and Stoddard.

I knew what to do if captured – name, rank, serial number, and nothing else.

The truth was, I was scared spitless and we'd all heard the stories of the POWs and how no Geneva Convention was going to stop our enemy from torturing us and then dropping us in some mosquito breeding ground, dead, when it was all over.

None of us was commander.

We were just soldiers, and we had no valuable information at all, and no reason for a negotiation with our commanders.

BUT HOPE IS the last thing to go, and so we had it.

I had it, and Gup had it, although Stoddard had already told me that he knew he'd die in the jungle and he didn't give a damn because his girl was already pregnant by some other guy and his folks had disowned him for some reason he wouldn't say, and what the hell was the point?

That was his attitude, and even though I felt we lived on Ice Planet and life was a hurdle into chaos, I still hoped.

For the best. For life. For good to come out of bad.

I WOKE UP LATER ON, pain running through my arms and legs like they'd had nails driven into them. I crouched in a dark hole in the ground that smelled like feces and had just a grate at the top so I could see a little of the sky.

Luckily, I still had a pack of gum on me – I kept it in this small pouch at the back inside of my skivvies that my mother had sewn for me to hide money.

Instead, I hid Wrigley's gum there.

I took a sliver of a piece and began chewing it just to feel as if I were still an American and that things mattered even if I was in a hole in the ground.

I WAS a little boy when my mother taught me

the game, only it wasn't really a game the way she told me about it. It was a way to get calm and to try and get through pain. I guess I was probably four when she taught me it.

She said my grandmother had taught her, and that her grandfather knew about it, too.

It was like make believe, but when I had scarlet fever as a kid, I really needed something to help me get through it. I was sure I was going to die, even though I didn't know what death was at four.

But scarlet fever gave me an inkling.

※

I was feverish and delusional, and I remember being wrapped in blankets and taken in the car to Dr. Winding over in Palmerston, and lying naked on his ice cold metal table while his nurse drew out the longest needle I had ever seen in my life and they told me it wouldn't hurt, but I screamed and screamed and my mother and father had to hold me down while that needle went into my butt.

Even though I still had fever, it wasn't quite so bad. But my butt stung, and, wrapped in blankets on the way home, I was in my mother's arms, a baby again. She whispered to me to try the game, that's what she called it.

I named it the Dark Game later on. When it got to me.

At home, in my room, she sat beside my bed and told me to close my eyes despite my moans and groans, and she told me to take her hand. But I couldn't close my eyes. I kept opening them.

Finally she took a handkerchief and put it over my eyes like a blindfold. She began the rhyme. I said it along with her in a singsong kind of voice.

After a bit, she and I were somewhere else, in the woods, in darkness, and I could not feel the pain or the fever at all.

She told me that it was a way the mind worked that was like magic, that it got you out of yourself and out of where you were.

WHEN I BEGAN to teach my friends how to do it as a kid, she pulled me aside and told me that I should keep it to myself.

"Why?" I asked.

"Because it can be bad, too. It's important to stay in the world. To not delve into that too much. If you need God, there's church. If you need friends, don't go off into your head too much."

But I didn't understand what she meant then, and I'm not sure I do now.

Or maybe I do and I just don't want to look at it.

"It's a daylight game," she said. "Between you and me. It's a Raglan game. It's just to make things easier when they're rough."

I played it, all by myself, my eyes closed, that wintry day in the smokehouse when I shot my dog, too.

I played it in that hole in the middle of the jungle without a hope in hell of getting out of there alive.

THE FIRST DAY AND NIGHT, They watched me.

'*They*' being the enemy.

I don't want to call them what we called them back then. It was racist. It was nasty. It was a nasty place to be. I hated their guts.

They were Enemy.

They were *They*.

We were *Us*.

My boys – that's how I thought of Gup and Stoddard and Davy – screamed at night. I heard them clearly. I'm pretty sure Stoddard died right away.

That's what I heard, anyway.

I could picture him working hard to piss off the Enemy, even if his nuts were being nailed to the wall. Gup might hang in there. Davy, I worried most about. He was practically just a kid.

I began to discover my darkness in my dirty pit of a bedroom. I began to feel my environment.

I guess I was about twenty feet down. Some kind of well.

Maybe it had been dug up for water.

Or prisoners. I don't know. It was deep but not wide.

I HAD JUST enough room to sit with my knees nearly touching my chest. It was dirt and rock, and they lowered water down after midnight, just a cup on a string. Half the water had dropped out of the cup by the time it reached me.

Not even a cup, I discovered. A turtle shell. Drank out of it because I was damn thirsty, and I soon discovered that if I didn't drink out of it fast, they yanked it back up.

They.

Sons of bitches.

I stared up through the grate, trying to see

the stars or at least something that meant the hole was not just an o in the earth that had no beginning and no end.

§.

MEMORY:

Back to Texas, back to the night I got tied up, back when I was barely more than a kid and out on an adventure.

The girl who tied me up was named Genie, and she could be had in that sunbaked Texas town for less than twenty bucks.

I was too young to be sure what I could do with a girl like that – I had left my sheltered island a virgin of eighteen, and knew that I would have six months or so before getting my orders overseas into the heart of the war.

I didn't want to die a virgin; and I doubt there has been a virgin in existence that wanted to die in that state, untouched by another.

So, when my buddies and me went out to the local rat bar called *The Swinging Star*, playing pool and chugging too many beers, I let down my guard a bit when one of my friends, named Harry Hoakes, slapped me on the back and whispered in my ear with his sour mash breath that he and a couple of the guys were going down to Red Town, a part of the desert where the whores were cheap and fast and you could buy a few for a good deal less than a week's pay.

I look back with shame, of course, upon this youthful episode in my life.

I do not proudly admit that my first experience with a woman was at the hands of a seasoned pro of twenty-six, but it is what it is – or, it was what it was. I was drunk, stupid, pretty sure I was going to die in some distant jungle, so I went with my *compadres* out in a truck that some townie drove – no doubt the pimp for the Red Town girls.

We unloaded outside yet another bar, and went in, and there they were, like glittery fool's gold, or broken glass mistaken for diamonds on a moonlit highway.

Harry Hoakes looked like a movie star and was from L.A. and had this air of magic around him, no matter what he did.

He died in the war, within a year. I heard he stepped on a mine and it just ripped him up.

But that night, he was completely on and alive like lightning – all around you and illuminating the dark.

This landscape was alien to me – slovenly, lazily pretty girls who looked the way whores are supposed to, not quite unhappy yet with their situation, not quite sure of how they landed in that desert canyon, not quite hardened to the way their lives would surely go.

When you're eighteen and in the army, whores don't seem sad or needy or even lesser.

They seem like angels who don't ask for the reasons of your interest. They know you want them, and they're perfectly fine with that.

Harry Hoakes introduced me to the girls like they were his sisters. The one who sidled up to me was Genie.

"I'm like that old movie star, Gene Tierney. From *Laura*. You ever see *Laura*? It's a beautiful movie. I'm gonna be a movie star someday. I *am*."

She was a big brunette with big teeth, from the Midwest, she said, a farm girl who wanted adventure, and intended to wind up in Hollywood in a couple of months – some producer had discovered her already and she was just waiting to hear from him, she told me all of it so fast it made me laugh.

Then, she asked me what I wanted to do.

❧

WE GOT a bottle of Jack Daniels and went back to the motel and plunked down the few bucks for a two-hour stay.

After that, she brought out those ropes from

some little overnight bag she lugged around with her.

She told me that since I was a virgin, she wanted to make sure I didn't do any of the work.

That's what she called it, and I guess it was her work.

But when the ropes went on, I went off somewhere.

I was no longer in a rundown motel with a big toothed girl, but back on Burnley Island.

IT WAS WINTER (as my memories of that New England island often are in a hot, dry, desert place) and my father tied me up to the post that sat at the center of the smokehouse.

He told me I had been bad to do what I had done, and that he had to teach me a lesson.

I was, perhaps, fourteen, my shirt had been torn off my back, and I felt the sting of his cat – a cat-o-nine-tails that he kept to discourage my brothers and me from doing the bad things we often did.

But in my Dark Game memory, I didn't feel pain from the stings – I felt myself glowing, becoming a powerful creature beneath the lashes.

I felt as if I were commanding my father to whip me, to torment me with the bad things I'd been doing. I felt as if I were a god, and he were merely my servant.

And soon, in the Dark Game, it was my father with his shirt torn, tied to the post, and I had the whip, and I was lashing at him and telling him that he was a bad, bad man.

When I opened my eyes, the game done, I found that I was tied to that bed in the motel in Texas. Outside, the sound of trucks going by.

IN A CORNER OF THE ROOM, the a woman lay, a crumpled rag doll, her face bloodied.

HARRY HOAKES CAME A-KNOCKING at the motel room door. I was tied up in Room 13, which made it lucky, I guess.

He was drunk from his own bottle of Jack Daniels, and he nearly busted down the door to get to me.

INSIDE, he looked at me, tied up and naked on

the dirty bed, and then at Genie, her big teeth all but knocked out, lying in a corner, her eyes wide.

He stared at me, then at her.

"I passed out," I said.

"Jesus H." He scratched his head, dropping his nearly empty bottle. His fly was open from his time with his girl. He was too drunk to process everything. "What the hell?"

"I don't know. I passed out. We didn't even do anything."

"Must've been her pimp," he said.

"She's got a pimp?"

"What, you think she's a nice girl from Iowa?"

"Maybe she's not dead," I said.

"If she's not dead, then she's the greatest actress in the world. Because she's dead like I ever saw dead."

"She thought she was going to be like Gene Tierney."

"Who?"

"That pretty actress with the overbite. In *Laura*. You ever see *Laura*?"

He looked at me kind of funny, and then shook his head. "We are up the legendary creek, my friend. You got a dead whore in your room, and you're...well, naked as a jaybird tied up." Then, he let out a laugh.

"Christ, you could not have made this up if you wanted to."

"Help me out of these ropes," I said. "Houdini I ain't."

❧

IN THE HOLE, in the prison, the enemy would sometimes stand over the grate and spit.

They did this a lot, and now and then, they'd take a leak down on me. I'd hear *them* laughing up above.

This might've been happened over a few days or a few weeks. I barely saw the sun in that time, because the grate got covered by a board during the day. They didn't want me to get that Vitamin D from the few rays of the sun, I guess. It was like living in a cave, and time seemed to evaporate.

I lived in endless night.

They'd get me out of there sometimes, too. Usually when it was dark.

They'd send a rope down, and I was to bind my hands to it and they'd pull me up.

Why did I go?

They fed me during those times. Fed me much better than if I stayed in the hole and ignored the rope.

They brought me up and gave me fish or

frog or some kind of large maggot cooked with thick flat leaves around it that didn't taste half-bad to a starving guy.

They pretended to be friendly, and the one who spoke English, who I called Harry Hoax after my friend from Texas, because he sounded a little like the real Harry Hoakes, he made light jokes with me about my situation that actually were pretty funny.

So my new friend Hoax took me aside into the mud-brown cell where I'd get the sumptuous feast, and he told me that he was my only friend.

"Your men already betrayed you," Hoax said. "They have told the commander everything. The position of other companies. The plans of the General."

I looked at him, grinning. "I bet they have. Good for them."

"Yes," Hoax said. "It is good. How are you feeling? I see sores on your shoulder."

"I'm fine."

"You seem in good spirits. Are you praying to your god?"

"God has more important things to worry about than me."

"I bet you are thirsty."

"Somewhat."

"Good. We have some pure water for you.

And even a small cup of wine. Specially for you."

"To what do I owe this sudden bout of hospitality?"

"We are not primitive people. We may live and fight among the trees and swamps, but we have a sense of culture. You are important to us. We want you happy and healthy."

"That's why you put me in a hole in the ground."

"War is evil. I know that. We know that."

"Am I talking to 'I' or 'We'?"

He laughed.

"Very good. Here," he said, glancing at the doorway.

A young attractive woman entered, a wooden tray in her hands. On the tray, a small porcelain cup, and beside it some palm leaves. Atop the leaves, more of the fried grub I'd had before, and then what looked like a rabbit's leg, also cooked.

After setting this down in front of me, she left and returned moments later with a jug of water.

"You see? We treat you well," Hoax said. "All we ask is that you tell us a few things. They are minor, unimportant questions, really."

"I thought my friends told all. I certainly don't know more than they do," I said.

Suddenly, I heard a wail from one of the other cells.

I tried to place the voice as one of my team, but I could not. I wasn't even sure it was human.

Hoax closed his eyes for a moment as if he didn't enjoy the sound, either. Then, he nodded to the girl with the jug. She rose and poured water into the cup.

I brought the cup to my lips and drank too fast. She refilled the cup; while I sat there with Hoax, she made sure I always had water.

"There is a small bit of opium in the water," he said, softly. "You have pain, and it will help with it."

"You're drugging me?"

He sighed. "I feel bad for the state you're in. It is just a distillation of the poppy. Not enough to make you crave it. Just enough to ease any physical torment you might be feeling."

After a moment, I nodded. "That's kind of you."

"You are different from the others," he said. "You are not like other Americans, Gordon. You have a deeper quality. We do not want to hurt you. We want to bring you into realignment with truth."

"Ah," I said, feeling a bit blurred around the edges. I assumed this was the opium.

Hoax began the routine questioning that had been done before, and I gave him the standard answer, which was no answer at all.

At the end of this, my meal finished, he sighed.

He told me that he wished me no harm but that the war would end with their victory and our defeat and that all my pain would be for nothing.

"Perhaps," I told him. "Or perhaps not."

Two interrogators came in. I recognized in their eyes the sadism I'd seen before. These were pleasure torturers.

I would be their toy for the night.

Hoax left the cell looking a little sad.

The interrogators bound my hands and ankles, and began to play a game that I believe is called, in torturing circles, the Thousand Scratches.

But it didn't matter what they did to my body.

I closed my eyes, and I could begin the rhyme I'd learned as a child:

Oranges and lemons say the bells of St. Clement's.

And then, my mind eroded into darkness: I returned to the smokehouse, tied to the post, with my father's cat-o-nine-tails snapping hard at my scarred shoulders.

MY FATHER and I had good moments, too.

He took me hunting and fishing. We spent idle summer Sundays out on a skiff that he'd borrowed from a friend down in the harbor, and he told me of his abiding love for the sea.

He took me on his occasional deep sea fishing voyages, and he brought me closer to him when my sister Nora drowned off the island, coming home from the mainland on a small boat when a storm hit.

My father pulled me aside and wept with me, the closest he'd ever come to showing genuine softness and true compassion.

If I felt something other than love for him, it was no doubt honor.

I hated him for the whippings, but I knew that some demon drove him to it. I was willing to take it for the building of my character.

PERHAPS THESE DAYS, people might call the

police if a boy were being whipped by his father. But in those times, not long ago, it was considered nobody's business outside of the family's own concern.

My father's demons were many, but he seemed to have an overzealous Christian sense of the Devil and of Angels and of saving his children from the Burning Fires of Hell.

He'd shout at me, while he whipped, that this hurt him more than it hurt me, and that angels and Jesus wept as the lash ripped against my skin but that if I were to go to heaven, I must repent of my sinful ways, of the bad things I had done, and I must turn to Jesus and to God's grace and His iron will.

I was, he told me, of the Devil.

※

OH, the bad things I'd done, they were truly bad, I suppose.

I smoked a bit, and I drank sometimes when I was far too young to drink liquor.

Once, I tried to set fire to the smokehouse, but only managed to burn most of the field nearby and many of the small thorny trees.

He had also caught me in the woods, in a way that a boy doesn't want to be caught, and that was part of my sin.

I deserved the whippings, and took them, playing the game to get through them, and then would spend a feverish night with my grandmother's salve all over my back to help speed the healing.

I honored and respected my father, even then, and I also thought of ways I might kill him someday.

But I never did.

ONCE I AWOKE from the game, after the interrogators – my impersonal demons – had left their scratches all over my too-thin body.

They returned me to my pit, to my dark filthy bed.

Sometime later – days, perhaps – I was brought out again.

This time, Hoax was not happy with me. It seemed that my comrades had not said as much as they'd wanted. It seemed that none of us was behaving.

This time, I was to have a night of theater, he told me.

"Might I have a bit of that opium water?" I asked. I might've begged. I liked the stuff and I wanted to make my time in this Hell as pleasant as possible.

"Perhaps after," he said, rather sadly.

I was brought into a cell lit by the wavering flame of a candle.

In a corner, my buddy Davy, *sweet little Davy*.

His eyes, swollen from beatings.

His jaw cracked.

A festering wound on his scrawny arm.

Ropes again. This time, on his wrists and ankles.

Four men held the ends of the rope.

"This is a play we call the Tug of War," Hoax told me.

Then, he began asking me questions.

Tears came to my eyes, but I had nothing to tell them.

❧

THE FOUR MEN tugged at the ropes and I heard Davy's bones pop, one by one, as they pulled, and his jaw dropped open, slack, but he was still alive.

Until one of the men pulled what seemed to be the forearm right out of Davy's skin.

Oh, but the game kicked in again, you see, at that point, and I missed most of the evening's entertainment by flying off to Burnley Island, by going somewhere I would be punished for my sins, but they were *my* sins alone and it was *my* punishment and no one else's.

꧁

WHEN I CAME out of the game, I was missing a finger and had no memory of it being taken or of the burning metal that had cauterized it to keep it from bleeding.

Hoax, however, told me the next time I was hauled up that I was a man of iron.

"You didn't make a sound. You seemed…"

"To be someplace else," I said.

He nodded. "Where did you go? The one you call Axeman was using a dull small scissor to cut off your finger. Why didn't you flinch?"

"Magic," I told him. "What's on the menu for tonight?"

"Menu?"

"Bugs? Rats? Frogs?"

"Oh," he said, smiling. "Supper. Well, tonight, we have a special treat. Tongue."

"Cow?"

"Pig. But it's very good. Wild pig makes a wonderful dish."

When I was finished with supper – and it truly was sumptuous compared to my previous ones – they brought another from my company, the scrappy little guy we called Gup.

As with the previous show with Davy, he had obviously been beaten, and perhaps his left leg was broken, also, for he hobbled in and nearly collapsed when the interrogators let go of his arms.

"Your friend cannot speak," Hoax whispered in my ear, like a mosquito circling. "He has, unfortunately, just this afternoon, lost his tongue under the Axeman's blade."

Now, Hoax didn't say that the tongue I had just eaten was my buddy's.

He didn't have to.

Maybe it was, and maybe it wasn't.

But he obviously wanted to give me that message, no matter what the truth of it might be.

I didn't eat for a few days more, but finally, pulled out of the hole again, I gobbled down the food they brought me – a stew made from strips of meat and leaves that tasted terrible but completely satisfied the gnawing in my gut.

Again, Gup was brought out, this time missing both hands, cauterized and bandaged at the wrist.

"His hands fell like leaves from a dying tree," Hoax told me.

"Very poetic," I said, trying to keep my mind from thinking about Gup and the Axeman too much, and forcing myself to keep out of drifting into the Dark Game.

To remain in the moment.

"Have you ever tasted human flesh?" Hoax asked.

I looked at poor Gup's face.

I wished him to die right there. I prayed to God. I prayed to the Devil. I prayed to the Queen of Heaven, Mary, the Mother of God, *Blessed is the Fruit of her Womb, Jesus.*

I prayed that his spirit would be pulled from his body before another night passed.

This entertainment of Hoax's went on for several nights, but each time I refused to answer his questions.

I WILL ADMIT with nothing but shame that I began to crave the meals brought to me, and I convinced myself – no doubt for survival's sake – that this was *not* the body of Gup that I slowly consumed, sliced from him day after day and cooked up with spices and aromatic flowers to make dishes that I began to love.

This was simply meat that had been taken from the body of pigs and rats and snakes and lizards and frogs and fish and other creatures of this Enemy's country.

This, a steamy bowl before me, did not hold Gup's foot, sliced into slivers, swimming in fragrant soup.

This was *not* a bit of flayed skin from Gup's buttocks, wrapped within an elephant ear palm leaf that had been buttered and baked into a moist but crunchy crust.

Yet, nightly, Gup was there, before me.

Soon an eye was gone, then his nose, his ears, toes and left foot, his lips sliced off, until I saw him no longer as a man at all, as a friend, as a former buddy, as one of the team.

I saw him as the supplier of my life.

IN A DREAM, in the hole, I had a vision of the great snake of life, devouring its own tail.

Life eats life, the image of the snake seemed to tell me. Life devours itself. You are part of this, and so is Gup. The snake is the whip in my father's hand. The whip is in my hand and reaches from my bloodied back to whip my father's hand. The torturer and the tortured are each playing a part and cannot be without the other.

I awoke from this dream and knew then that life was neither beautiful nor perfect nor magical.

Life was simply the gutter of heaven, the place where offal and waste stagnated, encircled with pestilence.

I BEGAN to love my suppers with Hoax.

Even when the Axeman came to me, a razor in his hand, and my mind shooting off to the game, I began to enjoy my contact with these cosmic barbarians and I looked forward to whatever they had in store.

I had forgotten my army, my country, and my friends.

There was only my hole and my cell, and my smokehouse back on my beloved home island.

It was the whole universe, and I could not tell whether it was heaven or hell.

Then, coming from the Dark Game out into the cell again, it was pain in my crotch that had me screaming, yet I felt distant from the scream.

I felt I could measure the scream and how it flew along the cell walls, bouncing up and down and back again.

They took another one of my fingers, but worse, one of my nuts was felled that night.

The Axeman had done it with his little razor.

I hadn't answered the questions and they had taken my left ball after slicing off my next finger down from my already-torn-off pinkie.

When I came around, I was in the cell, screaming, and one of my guys – Larry Pastor – sat across from me, watching me, his face trembling as if with an impending storm of sobs.

I had become the new entertainment for someone else now.

I was the star of the show.

THE NEXT NIGHT, I had the best supper yet, with Larry staring at me from across the room, his face a grimace.

What was I eating? My finger? My testicle? Or simply some special sliced rat over a bed of eel-leaves?

"It's all right," I told him. "It tastes good. It really does."

I WASN'T sure what I ate most nights, but the

strangest thing of all was that I had begun gaining weight.

I still drank a bit of the opium water – Hoax would bring in barely a thimbleful. I guess he wanted to keep me pliable yet sober enough when necessary.

I attributed my gain in bulk to a combination of the fatty meat they fed me, as well as sitting in a hole in the ground for days on end.

Hoax commented on my healthy look and I could see it in Larry Pastor's eyes – while he got thinner and thinner, no doubt refusing to eat any meat offered him, I was beginning to pack on the pounds.

Truth was, I felt better.

I felt as if my mind had adjusted to the hole and the cell.

I began to realize that, contrary to what Hoax might've thought, I never even felt I was going to escape. I just refused to tell Hoax or his beloved Axeman any military plans or secrets because I knew that once I told, I was as good as dead.

The meals would stop.

They'd leave me in the hole and either forget about me completely, or fill it in with dirt and rocks.

I began to see my imprisonment as a kind of luxury hotel – a fancy five-star place.

I began living in my head a lot, believing that I went on adventures when I was in the hole. I used the Dark Game to get out – I began to see the world again.

❦

I WAS IN PARIS, briefly, for a moonlit walk along the Seine with a beautiful girl who reminded me of a teacher I'd once had a crush on.

I ate a delicious breakfast on the Champs-Élysées, buttered almond croissant and a demi-tasse of espresso while watching traffic as it headed toward the Arc de Triomphe.

Another voyage out, I sat upon a striped blanket along the beach of some tropical island, surrounded by bare breasted beauties. I feasted on juicy mango and velvet coconut milk, feeling warm breezes as the shadows of palm trees cast thin lines along the pumice-strewn sand.

In the cell, I'd go to Burnley Island, to a moment in the past; but in the hole, I'd be somewhere magnificent, off on some adventure that was like a wish fulfillment of my boyhood.

Perhaps this saved me.

Perhaps it damned me.

❦

IN MY RARE moments of lucidity, I'd try to stay grounded by chewing on a small bit of the Wrigley's gum – the little I had left. A tiny infinitesimal piece. It reminded me of who I was, where I was, why I was there.

I began to talk to Hoax, without even knowing that I might be giving away secrets.

I TOLD him all kinds of things. Not military secrets. Just about my life.

About my nocturnal adventures.

Hoax became my best friend, and I suppose months passed.

Other soldiers were captured. Sometimes I saw their faces, and now and then I recognized them.

But they were part of the *Show* now. I watched the Show, or they watched me in their version of the Show.

But Hoax didn't let the Axeman cut from me again.

MY PERFORMANCES for the horror of the new recruits tended to be drawn from the contortionist's trade. My limbs were pummeled and pulled and twisted.

I felt none of it, off in my game.

I was valuable. I began telling things here and there. Nothing important, of course, but I'd become quite a good storyteller as I gained weight from my substantial meals.

My tales of wonder and awe for my host, the polite Mr. Hoax, were about life outside of the jungle, and he loved these adventures into other worlds. He had studied the works of Shakespeare, so now and then we'd talk about *Macbeth* or about *Othello*, and I told him about *Moby Dick* and how my island was somewhat like Nantucket and had been part of the whaling trade.

He loved American movies, too, so we talked about them at some length, and he offered up critiques that were quite well-thought-out about how Americans approached movies as opposed to other cultures. He also enjoyed discussing famous wars, and warriors of the ancient world.

THESE CONVERSATIONS often went on during the torture of another countryman of mine, usually roughly my age, once handsome, once with dreams and a sense of goodness of the world, all of them still having some meat on their bones.

I watched a man weep as the Axeman sliced off both of his ears, and then held them high for me as if ready to toss them to a trained seal.

I am ashamed to admit that, deluded and not really as sane as I should've been, I clapped for this performance because I thought it was some kind of special effects magic.

The Axeman was good at his job.

I had no idea what Hoax had in store for me, but soon enough, he brought me into a lower level of Hell with him.

HERE's the thing about the Dark Game:

By itself, it's simply a mind trick. It's a way to open doors inside you and to escape. Pain. Hurt. Sorrow.

That's all it is.

But in that prison camp, with the techniques they taught purely by trying them on me, I learned how to add another level to the game.

How to make it go deeper.

And when it did, something truly magnificent came of it.

"Brainwashing."

It sounds like some medical experiment.

But it's really simple.

You just put the subject in a position of separation from every sensory detail.

And then you go to work on him.

I had been prepared for it, in my training.

But I guess you're never really prepared for this kind of thing, not after months in a hole in the ground, not after watching your friends get their noses and eyes and ears and hands cut off in front of you.

Not after they feed you what might be your left ball.

Hoax had me bound up, hands in front of me, but tied to another rope that went to my ankles.

They positioned me, standing, in the middle of a cell.

Plugged a fan into the wall. I guessed this was to help block out any noise beyond the cell wall.

Then, each wall was covered with a dark

cloth to block out even the cracks of light that might come in.

Additionally, Hoax tied a blindfold around my eyes.

Plunged into absolute darkness, I felt Hoax touch my hands.

"You are going to be here for several hours," he said. "You are not going to touch the wall. Or sit down. Or fall. Should you fall, you will be strung up so that you are dangling from the ceiling with a stick thrust between your arms to keep you balanced.

"So, do not fall, that is my advice, my friend. You are to keep silent. If you cannot keep silent, our mutual friend Axeman will cut out your tongue and sew your lips together. Understood?

"This is for your betterment. We find that you are truly a patriot to the world, to freedom, and to honor. We want you to realign yourself with nature and man's true calling, instead of with this monster you have served in America. You have been deluded by your country, and we intend to help you recover. You are special to us, and to me, Gordon. You are worth realigning. I consider you my friend."

These were the last words I heard for many hours, during which my bones ached, my bowels let loose without my being able to control them.

After awhile, I felt as if I were floating.

The sound of the fan – a buzzing like a thousand black flies – seemed to take over my mind, as if it were what my brain generated: the noise of a cosmic buzzing.

Somewhere beneath it, after awhile, I heard Hoax's voice again, only I could not make out what he was saying.

I was fairly certain, however, that he existed inside my head, washing my brains the way he might wash his hands with a feminine delicacy, planting ideas and truths known only to the Enemy, trying to make me over into one of his house servants.

I went into the Dark Game. I heard Hoax clearly inside the game itself. I understood how this brainwashing could serve the Dark Game – and how it could help me survive.

GETTING into your brain isn't the problem with brainwashing. Anyone with a good mental crowbar can unlock that mush of gray matter.

It's making your mind separate from your body so completely that your body becomes a servant to someone else's mind.

That is the goal of brainwashing.

They are not cleansing the brain. They are turning it off, and switching on another brain, imprinting another set of memories and values and thoughts so that your past is no longer there.

It is wiped out, but not so completely – you think you are the same person. But someone else has invaded you.

The Other. The one who has turned off one switch has juiced you from another one.

And you are that person's mind now. You are that person's imagination.

That is what I learned. That is how I began to understand that the Dark Game was not just for one to go off on flights of fancy. To protect you from some pain of life.

It could be changed, using this brainwashing.

❦

IT COULD BECOME a way to turn a switch in another – to implant your own mind into another's mind, so that he no longer had his own perception but might, at least briefly, have yours.

I knew there was a way I could use this on Hoax.

On the Axeman.

❧

I KNEW that there was a way I could put the Dark Game into them so that I might escape.

❧

THEY TOLD me later that I stood there for twenty hours.

They told me later that I had been realigned.

But I had not been.

The Dark Game had saved me. It had protected me. It had kept me from letting their words and thoughts press into my gray matter.

When they brought me out into the sunlight – for the first time in many months – they rejoiced and called me *Comrade* and *Friend* and *Healed One*.

But, on the inside, I had already begun planning how I would destroy them, set their camp on fire, and sow the ashes with salt so that those demons might never rise again.

❧

BUT I'VE GOT to pull you back to that night

when I was young and in a bad part of some Texas town.

Remember?

Me, tied to the bed, the dead whore on the floor and the real Harry Hoakes, my buddy, my pal, untying me, his breath all whiskey and perfume absorbed from his girl for the night.

"She thought she was going to be like Gene Tierney," I said, and then, "Jesus, I'm going to end up in jail for this."

"Or you'll be in the jungle. In the goddamned war. Which do you want?"

"I choose the goddamned war."

Harry grinned, slightly, despite everything. "You didn't do it. You were tied up. I'm a witness to that."

I got up and got dressed as fast as I could, tripping over my trousers as I yanked them up.

"You let her tie you up?" He laughed.

I shot him a glance that shut him up.

"What are we going to do?" He said.

"We ain't gonna get caught, that's for damn sure," I said.

Next thing I remember, we're dragging that body out to Harry's car, and we plop her in the trunk.

I looked at her once, in that fizzling little light of the trunk, before we shut it down on her.

Her face.

She was somewhere else.

That's what Death is, I thought. It's going into the Dark Game for good.

I had no feeling for her. She was no longer there.

But the drive out to the mesa, thirty miles away from Red Town, the whole way I kept wondering how she had been murdered, and why I woke up from the Dark Game with the strange feeling of pleasure in my loins as if I had truly lost my virginity that night.

But that remains a Mystery with a capital M.

Part of me has felt all these years that I had untied myself, had beaten her to death, and then had somehow wrapped myself up in the ropes again.

Houdini, after all.

WE BURIED her in a desolate spot, so deep that the coyotes and scavengers wouldn't be able to dig her up.

I heard, years later, that Red Town eventually flourished and became more than a saloon and whorehouse railroad stop. It expanded out into the mesa.

I think that at some point a shopping mall was built near that grave of the girl who thought she looked like Gene Tierney and kept a rope in her overnight bag.

❧

HARRY SAID TO ME, at four that morning, driving back to base, "No matter what happens, we can't ever say we met her. Or were even there. The other girls won't tell. They don't like cops. But you and I have to be clear on this. We were never there."

"Where?" I asked, and then Harry muttered, "Jesus," and I knew our friendship was over that morning.

When I heard he died later, in the war, I felt bad for him. I missed him, too. We had done our time together, and that's a bond that remains even after death.

I wonder if he ever got over the sight that had greeted him when he stepped out of the ordinary world of red light night and into that motel room of me tied up and a dead woman on the floor.

But now, he's in the Dark Game.

❧

Suddenly, like an overnight celebrity, I became revered among the Enemy in our camp.

No longer made to sleep in the hole, I had a straw mattress beneath me, and I ate regular food with some of the lower officers.

More of my own countrymen arrived at the camp. I observed them as they trooped in, proud and wounded. Some of them spat at the ground as they marched by me.

The camp spread across a flat wetland area with long planks laid across muddy ground, rising to low hills where most of the buildings sat, and behind which on a kind of plateau, dotted with the holding wells for prisoners.

The commander's headquarters sat at the highest point of one of the hills, and I got to calling it Mount Olympus. The pits and holes where the Americans were kept, I called Tartarus.

I taught Hoax about the various levels of Hell, and he and I cooked up a scheme to begin a new set of torments for my countrymen.

We would take *Dante's Inferno*, which was

easy enough to find even with the supposed anti-European sentiment of the Enemy and from it create elaborate Rings of Hell for the prisoners.

Next, I talked about the cannibal torture. I suggested a whole new way to do this.

Why even use the Axeman? For despite his pleasure in the art of cutting flesh and bone from a live victim, wouldn't there be a more effective Host of such theatrics?

Why not *me*, their countryman?

What would be more horrifying than a well-fed compatriot slicing off the lips of his fellow American in front of the remnants of a once-proud platoon?

A USO show from Hell, I called it. We'll make it a grand show, a hot ticket in the hot jungle. A feast for the eyes and ears. We'd entertain Hoax's soldiers, as well as mesmerize my American friends.

It took Hoax several days to see this as the grandiose and intriguing idea that it might be.

But then he smiled and nodded. "Yes, my friend Gordon, this might be quite a wonderful and acceptable entertainment."

The USO Show from Hell would begin.

WE'D HAVE beautiful girls dancing for the boys.

Then, we'd have the main event. I'd do a comedy routine, I told Hoax.

I'd strip them of their dignity. I'd cut off bits and pieces of the happiest, sweetest guy they knew, the youngest of their friends, the ones they thought of as mascots and baby brothers.

Right before their eyes.

"They'll tell you what you want to know," I said. "They'll divulge their mother and father's addresses if you want, once we do this."

Hoax, not suspicious in the least, was thrilled.

Yet, he still didn't completely trust me, for he felt the Axeman should be there to do the slicing.

I wasn't to be handed knives or razors. I was still a prisoner, albeit a *Friend of Our Country*, as they proclaimed loudly, nightly, into the pits and holes of Tartarus, making sure that every single captured American soldier knew my name and where I'd been born and what I'd done for my newly adopted fatherland.

Once everything was set, the prisoners began building the stadium.

I OVERSAW ITS CONSTRUCTION, and they

worked tirelessly and swiftly, for I told them that it was a monument to their Dead.

That it was their Memorial and that they must take pride in it.

I spent some nights with them, talking of how we were going to be well-treated by our captors, and that they must trust me, despite appearances.

They didn't trust me at all, I could tell, but they had the resignation of those who wait for freedom to come from outside their sphere. The helicopter raids from the sky, perhaps, they hoped. The end of the war itself was not too much to wish for in their current state.

They had lost all will to escape. They were broken, yet capable men.

They did as I told them to do.

I also spent nights with them, playing the Dark Game.

I needed their minds. I need to bring them into a state of calm and of service.

I needed for them to hear only *my* voice among all the voices of their prison.

The bleachers went up, the theater backdrop created.

WITHIN TWO WEEKS, it was, by the standards

of the jungle, a beautiful imitation of an amphitheater, and could seat forty or fifty men.

The night of what I called *The Most Magnificent Show in the Universe*, finally arrived.

A banner announcing this, painted from human blood, hung from the wall.

❧

THE CELEBRITIES of our Damnation were there: the Commander, with his long face and inscrutable gaze; my friend Hoax, a chubby, round-faced fellow who whispered in the Commander's ear, no doubt about the show to come; the Enemy soldiers, dressed as if for an evening at the theater.

No doubt the women with some of them were not wives, but girlfriends who lived in the nearby Enemy Town, just beyond our Doom City.

The girls had fine red or blue dresses on, as if they would go to a celebration after the show. The men were dressed in full military garb. Cocktails were served, a rarity at this outpost, but the liquor had been distilled from a local flower, and left behind a scent in the air like jasmine.

The atmosphere fairly crackled with the electric moment to come.

I felt as if we were going to stage a great Broadway show. Or a spectacular Fourth of July fireworks demonstration.

It would be, I was certain, the inauguration of some wonderful event that might be remembered and talked about for years to come.

Was I nervous? Of course. How could I pull off such a scheme? What if I were found out? What if something went wrong? If one thing had gone wrong, one tiny thing, all of it would fall like dominoes and it would make stepping on a mine seem like a walk in the park.

THE USUAL EXCITEMENT of opening night spread, even among my countrymen. They were brought in, roped at the hands, shackled at the legs, shuffling to their seats, although I kept a contingent backstage, those American actors in the drama to unfold.

Footlights consisted of small fatty candles laid in a semi-circle around the stage floor.

The backdrop, an enormous canvas that had once been an officer's tent covering but was now painted with scenes of the Enemy's Great Leader, stepping on all symbols of the USA. There was a ragged Statue of Liberty crumbling, there Uncle Sam, blinded and toothless his top hat a wreck, and there along the edges was our president being corn-holed by one of our great generals.

Just seeing the backdrop made the Enemy guard cheer and raise their glasses.

What they didn't know, of course, was that I had made sure that a quite a bit of the opium water that I had grown to know well was stirred into their drinks.

I led them in their national anthem. They stood and sang bravely and happily, they drank – all, including the girls – I could tell from their expressions that they had begun to go into a blurred state – the strong alcohol and the poppy milk made themselves known.

As the crowd quieted, and the lights came up, I announced from my perch at the edge of the stage:

"We are gathered here for a momentous occasion! This is the inauguration of a great moment of historical significance!

"We are all the proud and the brave who have learned so much from our new masters, our friends and who wish to teach us the error of our ways and the true path of life! Here, on this very stage, you will see the wonders of transformation!

"You will see the magic of the ancients! The famous tricks of the fakirs of India! The secrets of the alchemists of old Europe! The mystical wonders of the sorcerers of ancient Mesopotamia!"

I spouted all the bullshit I could, and Hoax stood up and translated every word for the Enemy. They laughed, and brawled while some of my countrymen portrayed the President and our military leaders. They tripped, simulating intercourse with each other, acting like buffoons and idiots, all at my command.

The laughter from the stadium was enormous, even from Americans, whom I had brought into a state of the Dark Game just for this evening.

Hoax probably laughed the hardest, and once, when I glanced up at him, I saw the Enemy Commander slap him on the shoulder and whisper some approval in his ear that made Hoax beam.

The dancing girls came out next – they writhed and gyrated for the men. I had given them unhealthy doses of the local drink, and they began touching each other and taking off their clothes until they were nearly naked. This got the Enemy to cheer further, and the girls threw garments up to them.

My own countrymen sat quietly, as I had commanded for them to do in the Dark Game.

I could see that their eyes were glazed over, and they awaited my word.

Finally, to the delight of all, I announced the evening's entertainments.

"Tonight, good gentlemen and ladies, for your pleasure, the Axeman and I will carve up several Americans before your eyes. They will devour one another, as that is the way of our kind, and you will see how corrupt in our very beings we truly are. But first, I ask for volunteers from among you. For I want you to participate greatly tonight. Do I have any takers?"

The Enemy ranks roared approval, and many leapt from their seats to volunteer. But I wanted a special man to come forward. I wanted an important man.

"Commander!" I called out.

"Yes!" cried my countrymen, "Commander!"

Hoax laughed, clapping his hands, turning to his leader.

"Commander!" he said.

THE COMMANDER SHOOK his head violently, laughing the entire time.

While he resisted coming forward, I brought the few remaining men from my own company out on the stage. They were further along in the Dark Game than the other prisoners.

Each was blindfolded, and they held each other's hands. I had spent four nights with the three of them to make sure that their minds were switched into another realm, so that my voice and my mind was their only guide.

"Commander!" I cried out again, and even the Axeman, coming up beside me, raised his glinting blade as it caught the last of the sunlight and called the Commander by full name.

❦

FINALLY, goaded, blurred from drink, the Commander came down from the bleachers.

I raised a hand and called out a word of cheer, and all the Americans began clapping for him, and soon the guards clapped as well, whistling, as their beloved leader stepped up on stage.

"We have a magic show tonight!" I shouted to the noisy audience. "But we must have silence, now! Absolute silence!"

Within a minute or two, those in the bleachers quieted.

I glanced up at Hoax who smiled and nodded as if watching his prize protégé.

§

I THOUGHT of my friend Harry, blown to bits by a landmine. I thought of little Davy, tortured in front of me, tortured until his last breath left him.

I crouched down at the edge of the stage and blew out more than half the candles.

The sun had begun its descent and a gradually-creeping darkness seeped in like a dreadful mist.

Only six or so candles remained flickering, providing scant illumination to our stage. It was an effect I'd worked on – the backdrop now seemed ominous and evil – the Commander's face on the backdrop seemed to have gone in shades into a diseased, corrupt form rather than the healthy look that backdrop had when sunlight was upon it.

The crowd quieted even further, although I heard murmurs among the Enemy that set my teeth on edge.

They had begun to feel uneasy.

THE COMMANDER STEPPED up next to me, and patted me on the shoulder.

He announced to the crowd that I was a shining example of the realignment procedure that had been developed in the Great City.

I told the Axeman that it was time to begin the carving of the Americans.

He brought the blade up to the ear of one of my boys.

I STOPPED HIM, and announced, "Why an ear? Can you make a good purse from it, ladies?"

A tittering came from the women in the bleachers as if this were the cutest of jokes.

"I think not! Why not flay him alive? Right now? But even better, see how his friends," I pointed to the other two men, "don't know what's to come? Their ears are stuffed with wax. Their eyes are covered! Why not have them skin their friend for the delight of the Commander?"

Cheers went up, as I had expected.

In the dark, of course, it was the Americans who began the cheer, but in a stadium, cheers and claps become contagious. People want to be enthused about a show, and so the Enemy began crying out for more.

Then, when they quieted, I asked the Axeman for his blade.

Now, this was the point when my nerves nearly destroyed what I was about to do.

What if?

I felt sweat break out along my back. If he didn't pass me that weapon, none of this would work. If the drinks and the crowd didn't work on him, if he suspected anything...

THE AXEMAN GAVE me a strange look, but his commander, the Supreme Leader of the camp, nodded to him, and shouted in their language.

The pressure of an audience watching did exactly what I wanted it to do – the Commander was caught up in the magic of the theatrical moment. He wanted the show to go on as planned.

Reluctantly, the Axeman passed me the blade.

It was heavy, and its edge was sharp.

"YOU WILL NOW SEE," I announced, "one of

the Corrupt Americans be skinned before you, and before your Commander, by his own compatriots!"

The audience went silent as I passed the blade to one of my blindfolded men.

Quickly, however, I took it back, and whispered to the three men whose ears were not, in fact, blocked, "Now. To your left."

I turned with the blade, and stabbed the Axeman in the groin, and then cut my way up into his belly and sternum –

As the audience began to gasp –

The three men, blindfolded, grabbed the Commander and tore at him as if they were wild dogs.

꩜

IN THEIR HEADS, they were wolves, in fact, and they believed that they were tearing at a stag in the hunt.

The commander screeched, but the men were strong, and in the darkness of the stadium, the Enemy rose, panicking, but it was too late.

They had drunk the opium and liquor, and my countrymen had already risen up with gnashing teeth and a strength that they had never known they'd had in their bodies.

I wanted to see Hoax one last time, to see

the look on his face when he knew that this had not gone his way. That he had misplaced any trust he had in me.

But I couldn't find his face in the confusion.

I heard what sounded like wolves tearing at bleating sheep in the dark.

❧

THE BEAUTY of the escape of my men – men from various platoons who now thought of me as their hero – was that none could remember the show at all.

By dawn, not all the prisoners had survived. Many had died in the fight.

But those who lived, blood on their faces and blotching their clothes, awoke without memory of the past year.

They didn't know the atrocity committed against them, neither did they know of their own savagery, which had killed the Enemy in the camp.

By dawn, I commanded the men, still under the influence of the Dark Game, to set fire to the last of Hell.

❧

AN OLD MEMORY: I was sixteen, and my father lay dying in his bed.

My mother, who had to take up work now, needed me home to help nurse him while he was in pain.

I sat each day with him, and one morning, when I brought his breakfast, which he barely touched, he told me, "You're an evil son-of-a-bitch, Gordie. You show the world how good you are, but I know who you are on the inside. I've seen it since you were a baby. You have the Devil in you, and you spend your time hiding it."

I sat with him, patiently, nodding so that I might not appear to be the bad child.

Then, when he was through talking about my evil and how I was going to Hell, I offered him a glass of water.

He drank it, greedily, and passed the glass back to me.

"I still love you, dad," I said.

"I know you do," he said.

In the afternoon, he died, peacefully, in his sleep.

I missed him terribly.

His lifeless body, in that bed, made me remember the day he had me shoot my dog and had taught me about how sometimes, Death could be a friend.

THERE. I've told you it all.

I've told you about the war, and the young woman, and my father.

My youth, pulled from the drawer, so you can look at it and judge me.

I should be tied up.

Bound.

Whipped.

It is the only way for me to go out of this body, the freedom of my mind to wander.

It intensifies the Dark Game for me.

I don't want to remember anymore.

I want to close the drawer now.

I want to lock up the past.

I give to you, my wife, Mia, the key.

ABOUT THE AUTHOR

Douglas Clegg is the *New York Times* bestselling and award-winning author of *Neverland, The Priest of Blood, Afterlife*, and *The Hour Before Dark*, among many other novels, novellas and stories. His first collection, *The Nightmare Chronicles*, won both the Bram Stoker Award and the International Horror Guild Award. His work has been published by Simon & Schuster, Penguin/Berkley, Signet, Dorchester, Bantam Dell Doubleday, Cemetery Dance Publications, Subterranean Press, Alkemara Press and others.

A pioneer in the ebook world, his novel *Naomi* made international news when it was launched as the world's first ebook serial in early 1999 and was called "the first major work of fiction to originate in cyberspace" by *Publisher's Weekly*, covered in *Time* magazine, *Business Week, Business 2.0, BBC Radio, NPR, USA Today* and more. His book *Purity* was the first to be published via mobile phone in the U.S. in early 2001.

He is married, and lives and writes along the coast of New England.

Find the Author Online:
www.DouglasClegg.com

facebook.com/DouglasClegg
twitter.com/DouglasClegg
bookbub.com/authors/douglas-clegg